A DOUBLE
DETECTIVES
MEDICAL MYSTERY

DIAGNOSIS
DANGER

ROOPA FAROOKI

For Kiron Farooki,
my bossy, beautiful big-hearted sister.
Who is always right.
(She told me to add that last bit.)

And for all my hardworking colleagues in
the NHS—you are heroes.

OXFORD
UNIVERSITY PRESS

Great Clarendon Street, Oxford OX2 6DP

Oxford University Press is a department of the University of Oxford.
It furthers the University's objective of excellence in research, scholarship,
and education by publishing worldwide. Oxford is a registered trade mark of
Oxford University Press in the UK and in certain other countries

British Library Cataloguing in Publication Data
Data available

ISBN: 978-0-19-277361-6

1 3 5 7 9 10 8 6 4 2

Printed in Great Britain

Paper used in the production of this book is a natural,
recyclable product made from wood grown in sustainable forests.
The manufacturing process conforms to the environmental
regulations of the country of origin.

Images inside: The brain 'Christos Georghiou/Shutterstock'
Blood cells 'Oxford University Press'

A **DOUBLE DETECTIVES** MEDICAL MYSTERY

DIAGNOSIS DANGER

ROOPA FAROOKI

CHAPTER 1:
A PUDDLE OF BLOOD

'What!' yelled Ali. 'OMG, this is so TYPICAL of you!'

Tulip shrugged and carried on walking down the road. Holding her school backpack a bit tighter, like a back-shield. Just in case her twin did one of her trademark Ali-explosions and started throwing stuff.

'What's she yelling about?' asked Zac, running up behind Tulip.

'NO-NO-NO, this is UNACCEPTABLE!' carried on Ali, and she yanked off her backpack, chucked it to the ground, and started kicking it. Zac looked appalled, and stepped away cautiously, clutching his own over-stuffed end-of-term bags.

'TBH, could be anything,' said Tulip, sighing. It was pretty typical of Ali to make the short walk home from school into a big-budget drama.

Tulip looked at the bashed-up backpack on the ground. Reproachfully.

Ali looked at the bashed-up backpack on the ground. Mutinously. And then turned away, tossing her head. Chin so high in the air it was like it was competing with her nose.

'Shall I pick it up?' said Zac. His urge to be helpful had overcome his more sensible urge to stay away from Ali when she was approaching explode-mode.

'Don't you dare,' said Tulip, and she looked crossly at Ali. 'Pick-it-up,' she hissed. 'You're embarrassing me.'

'NO! *YOU'RE* EMBARRASSING *ME!*' Ali yelled wildly into the air, flinging her fists around.

Zac's too-tall twin brother, Jay, had caught up with them. He clocked the backpack, with Ali raging beside it like she was fighting a wasp, and plucked it from the ground.

'Guess you can't choose your friends,' he said practically.

'Not sure that's right,' said Tulip, frowning at Ali. 'It's *family* you can't pick.'

'Who's she yelling at?' Jay asked, shouldering Ali's backpack, and carrying on down the road with Zac and Tulip. 'Us?'

'I'm only carrying it to the end of your street,' he shouted back to Ali. 'Then I'm dumping it.'

Bizarrely, she turned to him and grinned. She even gave him a thumbs-up. And then, like a switch had been flicked, she went back to cross-face-screaming.

'Dunno,' said Zac, looking back at her doubtfully. 'I don't *think* I've been unacceptable today. Or embarrassing.'

'Not more than normal,' agreed Jay. 'You could have stopped volunteering for stuff. You make me look bad.'

'It's not *us*. She's on the phone to someone,' Tulip said, pointing to the white cords trailing from Ali's ears. 'She picked up the call when we walked out the school gates. But TBH it could be anyone. Ali's enemies list is long enough for bedtime reading.'

'I miss being on the enemies list,' said Jay.

'It was a lot less demanding than being on the bestie list.'

'Less fun, though,' said Zac. 'Being besties meant we got to skip class, foil a poison plot and save the school from Sprotland and his creepy-sleepy sickness.'

Tulip was about to say something mean about Evil Evelyn Sprotland, but managed to stop herself. It wasn't nice to be mean about people who were probably dead. Even if they were really bad people who wore stupid hats.

'NO! THIS IS NOT HAPPENING!' screeched Ali. 'You are so not doing this to me, MOTHER!'

The others stopped, shocked.

'Mother?' said Zac.

'Nooo,' said Tulip. 'This is bad. She used the M word. The OTHER M word. She only calls Mum that when she's really, really cross.'

'Don't-you-don't-you-DON'T YOU DARE HANG UP on me!' Ali shrieked. It was like waves of angry energy were coming off her. She was loud enough for local wildlife to fly startled into the sky, and run whimpering away up trees.

But one bit of wildlife raced towards her, instead. Like she'd made a cry for help. A scruffy black lump of fluff streaked up the road and wrapped itself around Ali's legs, purring affectionately.

'Not now, Witchy,' said Tulip, stooping to save the cat from Ali's flailing limbs. 'Poor dumb puss really can't read the room.'

'We're not in a room,' said Jay. He gestured around the slightly scabby, sunlit street, littered with bright weeds and after-school snack wrappers. 'Duh.'

'You know, I'm remembering why we didn't really like you before,' snapped Tulip. 'There's still space to get back on the enemies list.' She was normally nicer than this, but Ali's tantrum was beginning to get to her.

'Aww, you said *before*,' grinned Zac, picking up the stray crisp packets and taking them towards the bin. 'Means you really like us now.'

'NOOOOOOO!' shrieked Ali dramatically, yanking out her earbuds and flinging her phone away with a mic drop move, arm stretched out and fingers separated. Zac stepped forward and caught the phone with his spare hand, and for a moment they all stopped and stared at him, impressed by his reflexes.

''S nothing,' said Zac, shifting uncomfortably

under the attention. He dropped the litter in the bin, and gave Ali's phone to Tulip for safekeeping. 'Dad's super clumsy, I'm always catching the cutlery off the table.'

'I'm guessing she hung up?' Tulip said to Ali. The phone started buzzing again. 'Hey, Mum. Yeah, it's me. No, it didn't even hit the ground. Zac caught it.' There was a pause. A bit too long. 'Oh. Right. OK, Mum. Yeah, see you at home. Love you, too.'

'So what was all that about?' asked Zac, looking between Tulip and Ali.

'Beyond Ali's flair for the dramatic?' said Jay, handing Ali her backpack. She was giving Tulip a death stare.

'Love you, too?' she repeated mockingly. She shook her head in disgust. 'And I'll tell you what it's about. That woman, that MOTHER, has just cancelled the holidays.'

This was a big deal. The twins had been looking forward to half term. Mum had planned their first ever trip abroad, a few days in France, and had even got them passports. They were going to go on a plane for the first time. It was all they had talked about since the excitement of getting rid of their mum's evil boyfriend,

Brian Sturgeon the mad-bad brain surgeon, AKA frustrated fraud and identity thief, Evelyn Sprotland. He'd tried to poison his old school with a sinister sleeping sickness he'd cooked up, and when the twins had foiled him, he'd jumped off a bridge, escaping from the police. He was probably still in the river, as he'd never surfaced, and they'd never found a body. He wasn't missed at all. As Ali had said, pop goes the measle. And plop goes the weasel.

'Huh,' said Tulip. Sometimes she hated that she had to be the sensible, sweet one. Sometimes she wished she could just throw a big tantrum like Ali. She swallowed down her own disappointment, and patted her sister on the back.

'Well, I'm sure Mum didn't WANT to cancel the holiday,' she said.

She knew why it had happened. They both did. It was always the same reason.

It was the reason why someone else recorded their talking bits in the school assembly. Their bits on stage in the school play. It was the reason why someone else had always done the drop-offs and pick-ups. It was the reason why they started early and stayed late in the school clubs.

It had always been that way.

Tulip liked the idea that Mum operated on sick people, and made them better, but she didn't like that it seemed to take up so much of the day.

'Aww, sorry guys, that sucks,' said Zac.

'So why's your mum cancelling the hols?' asked Jay.

'Work,' said the twins together, glumly.

'You know you said that in creepy-twin unison,' said Jay.

'I'm too sad to come up with a cutting put-down,' sniffed Ali. 'So just make one up yourself.'

Ali's anger was swiftly dissolving into tears. 'It's NOT FAIR,' she muttered, stomping down the street, squashing the pavement-crack weeds and scattering the litter. 'We did all this cool stuff, we pretty much saved the whole school from a vengeful maniac, and we're the only ones who never get to have the holidays with our mum. And we've never gone away. We've never even gone camping.'

'We're not going anywhere,' said Zac. 'We can't. Mum's got her . . .'

'Chemo,' finished Jay.

Ali stopped sniffling. There wasn't anything

to say to that. She was itching to come out with something mean about how finishing each other's sentences was much creepier than speaking in creepy-twin unison. But even she knew that you couldn't compete in crossness with someone whose mum was having chemo. The treatment for Cancer. The big C.

'It's like it wins every time,' she muttered under her breath.

Tulip heard, and talked over her hurriedly.

'So both our mums are gonna be in the hospital through half term hols,' said Tulip. 'We can hang out there, if you like. There's the coffee shop with cakes, and the movie night and the . . .'

'Sick people,' added Ali. 'So many icky-sicky people.'

Jay laughed. 'You're not great at looking on the bright side, are you?'

They'd reached the end of the girls' street, and Ali sat on the wall outside the vet's, with her back slumped. Bugs and wasps crawled over the mushy fruit on the ground, that had fallen from the tree bulging out of the pavement. She pulled a small red fruit from one of the overhanging branches, and popped it recklessly in her mouth. It wasn't awful. She spat the stone out and watched it bounce to the kerb.

She didn't see the point in going home. Mum wasn't there. The neighbours' teenagers would be looking after them until she got back. They were alright. They had Nintendos and let them do the four-player mode on the telly. But they weren't Mum.

'I hate the holidays,' she said, kicking the wall. She thought about putting one of the tree fruits in her pocket, for testing, in case she got poisoning. But then she just reached for another, and glumly ate that too.

'Here,' said Tulip, with authority, handing her Witchy. 'Cuddle this.'

Witch sat like a heavy fluff-lump on her knees. Ali hesitated, and stroked behind the cat's ears. And then gave a brief experimental cuddle.

'It's like a troll doll came to life and got fat,' she sniffed, and then pressed her face into Witch's fur. 'Thanks, that helps.'

'Risky strategy,' commented Jay to Tulip. 'I'd have been worried she'd kick that, too.'

'It's not a *that*, it's a cat,' said Zac, sitting on the wall next to Ali.

'Bet *you're* great at looking on the bright

side,' Ali sniffed at him.

'Mum says I'm so good at it I should wear shades,' Zac agreed.

He propped up the brown paper bag full of all the arty stuff from the term that they'd cleared from their drawers, and put down the model of the Nile he'd been carefully carrying. Jay had somehow managed to carry both their working scales made with loo rolls and chopsticks, and a pair of delicate Venetian masks.

'Where's all your stuff?' asked Jay, noticing that the girls didn't have the regulation burst-to-the-seams plastic bags. 'Did you leave it at school?'

Tulip nodded. 'Yup, at school.'

Zac looked worried. 'But the cleaners might chuck all your artwork away!' He stood up. 'Let's go back for it.'

'Easy, tiger,' said Ali. 'That's kinda the point. Our stuff just ends up in the recycling, anyway.'

Jay was shocked. 'But . . . you mean, your mum just throws away your art?'

'Not just the art,' said Ali. 'The crafts and sculptures, too.'

'Not straight away,' said Tulip defensively. 'It sits in the kitchen for a while first. Or in our room until it gets covered by the clothes mountain.'

'Oh,' said Zac. He exchanged a look with Jay.

'What, like your mum keeps your toilet roll sculptures in a museum?' scoffed Ali.

'Not a museum,' said Zac just as defensively. 'We call it the gallery . . .'

'Mum put up a whole new set of shelving from Ikea to keep it in,' said Jay.

'Woman needs a hobby,' muttered Ali again. But this time, the boys heard.

'Hey!' said Zac, sharply.

'Hey yourself,' retorted Ali. She rounded on Jay, who'd placed a calming hand on Zac. 'You're feeling SORRY for us! Don't you dare!'

'It's OK,' said Tulip, wishing again that someone else would just say it was OK to her. 'It's not their fault the holiday got cancelled and we haven't got any place to keep the Venetian masks and the Nile.'

'Tweedledum and Tweedledumber are feeling SORRY for us,' grumped Ali. 'It's like rock bottom. This is the view from under the chocolate stain on the carpet.'

'Most people feel sorry for us,' said Zac, 'when they hear about Mum.'

'Yeah,' agreed Jay. 'It gets kinda tedious. We always get THAT face, you know, the sympathy face, with the head at a weird angle.'

'But at least our holiday didn't get cancelled,' said Zac, uncomfortable that they might be sounding competitive.

'Nah,' said Jay. ''Cause we were never gonna have one.' He said it flatly. No self-pity.

Ali saw her twin tilting her head with the exact sympathy face Jay had described, like she just couldn't help herself. She glared at Tulip, who caught herself and straightened up hurriedly.

Jay pulled open his bag, and yanked out a box tied with a real ribbon.

'OMG,' said Tulip. 'Are those your mum's special home-made biscuits? Thought they were for the teachers?'

'Mr Ofu didn't turn up today,' said Jay. 'He called in sick, but I saw him googling last minute hotels in Croatia yesterday at break. Reckon him and his boyfriend have bunked off for a good deal.'

'You snooze you lose,' agreed Ali, perking up. 'I approve of that.'

'You should have given them to the substitute,' said Zac reproachfully. He took the box and carefully undid the ribbon, and rolled it up. And then he neatly opened the box, without tearing into it.

'Mum made the box, too,' he explained.

''Course she did,' sighed Ali. 'Did she boil up the sugar-beet for the cookies, too?'

'Nope,' said Jay, ''Cause they're no-added-sugar.'

'No-added-sugar? Yum. That's Ali's favourite ingredient,' nudged Tulip. She was surprised when Zac held out the box to her first. She hadn't been the one shouting and crying.

She looked up at him, and he was beaming.

'It's OK,' he said. He took out the biggest cookie and gave it to her.

Tulip could have cried. She took the biscuit and bit into it. It was chocolatey and chewy and delicious.

'Your mum might be a magician,' she said.

A cab pulled up alongside them, honking noisily on the quiet street.

'Hello, my queens and kings!' called the driver, a smiling young man with teeth so white they looked luminous.

'Seriously, Momo. Do you brush with

plutonium or something?' Ali complained, covering her eyes from the glare. 'Put those things away.'

Momo was one of the local refugee kids their mum had mentored. She'd got him the cabbie job and sponsored him for uni. He was the one who'd usually drive them over to their Nan-Nan's, whenever Mum had to rush into the hospital to sort out brain surgery emergencies.

'Hey, Momo,' said Tulip, waving her cookie at him. 'You want some?'

'Most kind, but I am on duty,' he said, winking at her. She grinned and threw half the cookie into the cab, and he caught it, and put it on the lid of his re-usable coffee cup. 'Meet my friends, my dear lady,' he called courteously over his shoulder.

It took them a moment to notice that there was a pile of woman-shaped clothes on the back seat of Momo's cab. It was like someone had rolled down the clothes mountain in their bedroom and walked out with whatever had stuck. The woman was wearing a hideous hat, which looked like a few birds had died on top of it, with a net which obscured most of her face apart from a mean, lipsticked mouth.

'I am not your dear lady,' she harrumphed in a hoarse voice. 'You, you KNOW these people, do you? These wall-dwelling delinquents.'

'These delinquents are delightful, and I am their designated driver,' explained Momo politely.

'He is. He drove us all to the zoo a few weeks back,' added Zac.

'The zoo?' squeaked the woman, in an outraged voice. 'You, took THEM, to the zoo?'

'You never been?' asked Ali, trying to peer into the cab. 'You're sounding weirdly jealous.'

'Let me out, young man,' said the woman. 'You keep terrible company. I won't stay another moment in your cab. I'm getting the bus with a *respectable* driver.'

'Of course, dear lady,' said Momo with his usual over-the-top politeness that somehow never sounded sarcastic. He leapt out of the cab, and pulled open the lady's door for her, holding out an arm for her to steady herself. She shuffled out like a pile of rag-rugs, clomping onto the road and swiping a vicious-looking cane ahead of her.

'So, my regal young charges,' said Momo, turning to face them. 'The lady here does not lie. This wall is not your home.' He nodded to her as she went past him. 'Shall I accompany you . . . OW! Ow-ow-OW-EEE!!!'

Momo made a strangled cry, and toppled to the ground, face down. The old woman huffed and carried on clomping, faster, as though embarrassed by them all.

'Momo, quit kidding about,' said Ali distractedly, her mouth full of sugar-free cookie.

'OMG,' screamed Tulip. 'He's not kidding, look . . .' She jumped to the ground next to Momo.

There was blood streaming out of the back of his leg, drenching his jeans in thick, red goop.

'Get help!' yelled Ali, spitting out the cookie. The boys turned towards the woman, as the closest grown-up, but she had already hobbled to the end of the road, her hideous hat bouncing disdainfully as she turned the corner.

'Not her, you!' Ali pushed the boys off the wall. Jay stabbed his phone urgently to call for an ambulance. Zac kneeled next to Tulip on the rough pavement, and held Momo's hand.

Momo was breathing raggedly. 'My queens,' he seemed to be saying, almost apologetically.

'Shush, Momo, just breathe,' said Tulip,

adding, 'it's gonna be fine,' not knowing if it was a lie.

She was pressing down on the back of Momo's knee, where the blood was gushing.

'You got a knife?' asked Tulip, looking at Zac.

'What are you saying?' asked Zac, too shocked to be offended.

'I need a knife to cut off the back of his jeans,' said Tulip, 'I can't see where the blood's coming from.'

Ali pulled her keys out, and finding a hole in Momo's ripped jeans, tore them apart with the pointiest bit.

'It's there,' she said, yanking away the drenched denim. Tulip nodded, jamming her own knee right into the back of Momo's. The bleeding stopped as suddenly as switching off a tap.

But the puddle around Momo was still like something out of a horror movie. And the girls were covered in his blood.

It had only been three minutes.

'Where'd that woman go?' asked Zac. He was putting his blazer under Momo's neatly shaved head, grazed and bleeding from when he'd hit the pavement.

'Still hobbling towards her bus stop, probably,' said Jay, dismissively.

'Stupid old cow,' agreed Ali. 'Who walks off when someone's hurt?'

'Everyone in any public space, all the time,' said Zac. 'People don't like getting involved.' He said it with an un-Zac-like crossness. 'In case it gets in the way of their day.'

'I thought we were going to lose him,' said Tulip. 'That cut, it's in the popliteal artery. The deep one behind the knee.'

'How did he get a cut there?' asked Jay.

'With a blade,' said Tulip, bluntly. 'A really sharp one. Like a razor. And none of US have razors in our backpacks.'

'And only one person was near him when he fell,' added Ali.

And they all looked in the direction of where the mean old woman had limped off.

It was another agonizing minute before the ambulance roared around the corner, blue lights blazing. A pair of paramedics leapt out with a stretcher.

'Another victim of knife crime,' said the paramedic, sadly. 'Was he in a gang?'

'No. He's a social worker student,' said Tulip,

offended. 'And a part-time cabbie to put himself through uni.'

'It's always the good ones,' said the other paramedic, just as sadly. 'Rivalry, was it? Guessing the attacker couldn't handle the kid going straight. Did you get a look at him?'

'Her! It was a psycho pensioner,' snapped Ali.

Tulip shifted her knee, so the paramedics could do their work, and the blood started gushing again. Poor Momo groaned.

'We're going with him,' said Tulip, defiantly. 'We're his ride-along. He's not going alone.'

The paramedic looked surprised. 'You family?'

'Yes!' said both twins together.

The paramedics looked at each other doubtfully, but Ali looked too fierce to argue with, and Tulip seemed too sweet to be telling a lie.

'They're family,' confirmed Jay.

'Don't worry,' said Zac, 'we'll tell your babysitters where you are.'

When Momo and the girls were in the ambulance, Ali asked urgently, 'Momo, who was that client? Is she a regular?'

Momo shook his head, painfully slowly. 'She wanted to come to your street. She was waiting for a friend, she said. Just up the road. And then I saw you . . .'

'No more talking,' said the paramedic sharply. 'He's going straight to Resus in A&E.'

'Did you see her face, at all?' asked Ali. 'Her hair? Before she got that hat on?'

Momo blinked. 'It was red,' he said. 'Like a wig. A curly red wig.'

Ali and Tulip stopped in horror. A curly red wig. A woman in a curly red wig. A limping woman in a curly red wig.

'Nan-Nan?' they breathed.

CHECK PAGE 296 OF THE APPENDIX FOR THE MINI-MEDIX BLOG POST

EMERGENCY TWINTERVENTION! BIG BLEEDS OR HOW TO HINDER HAEMORRHAGE!

CHAPTER 2:
BODIES IN THE BEANBAGS

When Momo was stable and sedated in Resus, the girls noticed a stream of worried texts and missed calls from Mum.

'Guess we'd better call her,' said Tulip.

'We may as well see her,' said Ali. 'She's still in the building. She doesn't get off until 6 pm.'

'Will he be alright?' Tulip asked the nurse.

She smiled and nodded. The Emergency Department consultant in purple scrubs bustled up to them.

'You!' she said. 'Minnie's twins!'

'That's us,' said Ali.

'You girls probably saved this young man's life! How did you know how to stop the bleeding?'

'Mum said,' shrugged Tulip, 'use pressure. So I just dug my knee in there really hard.'

'So, was he stabbed?' asked Ali.

'Well, that would be a police matter,' said the consultant. 'But duh! The popliteal artery doesn't just pop out of the skin for a nice little jaunt because it fancies playing sprinklers for the day.'

'Lucky it wasn't the femoral artery,' said Ali. 'The bigger bit of pipework higher up the leg, that's why . . .'

'Butchers wear aprons,' the girls said together.

'Very good, girls,' said the consultant. 'Now where IS your mum?'

'Brain surgery,' said Tulip. 'Probably still in theatre. We'll find her.'

'Good, and don't worry. This young man will be right as rain. A couple of bottles of the house red will sort him out.'

'You're kidding, right?' said Ali. 'The house red? Alcohol's a horrible idea. And Momo's a Muslim, he doesn't drink red wine.'

'She meant packed red blood cells,' hissed Tulip. 'It was a joke.'

'Oh, I don't think so,' said Ali. 'Jokes are funny.'

They came out of Resus, and made it all the way out of the Emergency Department. But then they saw Mum rushing towards them down the corridor, still in her scrubs and mask, and with her blue net cap releasing her puffs of short hair.

'My babies!' Mum shrieked, ripping off her mask to kiss them and practically picking them up. The girls realized how they looked, like they'd been in a tomato splat fest.

'This is nothing, you should see the other guy,' said Ali, hugging her back. And then she remembered she was cross with Mum.

'Hey, no hugs and no my-babies!' she said, pushing Mum away, leaving an impressive smear of blood on her scrubs. 'What about the holiday?'

'Well, munchkin,' said Mum, 'I think that this afternoon has shown that it's far too dangerous for us to go on holiday anyway.'

'What?' said Tulip. 'But we saved Momo. He got attacked by some insane psycho . . .'

'Oh no, sweetie,' said Mum sadly. 'You can't use psychosis like an insult. It's a disease.'

'Is *mean* a disease?' said Ali, ''Cause she called

us delinquents and stabbed Momo in the back of the knee with her pointy cane.'

Tulip slapped Ali on the back. 'We're kinda burying the big news here,' she whispered. 'We've gotta tell Mum.'

'Tell Mum what?' asked Mum.

'We know who Momo's attacker was!' said Tulip. She couldn't believe that she was saying this. 'It was, well, we think it was . . .'

She paused. She couldn't bring herself to say it. But Ali could.

'Nan-Nan!' she cried out.

Mum looked confused. 'You can't mean . . .' she started to say.

But then she saw Ali was pointing down the corridor. The familiar hum of wheels on the speckled plastic of the hospital flooring. Nan-Nan was approaching in her black and silver wheelchair with go-faster black and silver stripes. She was subtle like that. She looked immaculate in her skinny jeans and leather jacket, with her diamond nose piercing, and her black and silver hair flying back in waves. Mum looked relieved and waved to Nan-Nan. She thought that Ali had just been greeting Nan-Nan in her usual dramatic way. Not accusing her glam granny of a terrible crime.

'OMG,' whispered Tulip.

'Oh-My-Nan-Nan,' corrected Nan-Nan, rolling up towards them. 'Damn, darlings, I thought I'd booked your babysitters. Thought I'd have a night off from clearing up your messes.'

'*Our* messes?' choked Ali. 'Think we BOTH know whose mess this is.'

Nan-Nan frowned, 'You're blathering, sweetie, you should really work on that.'

She looked them up and down. 'Red suits you,' she grinned. 'Are you in a play, or did you have a ketchup clash?' She pulled out her bright red lipstick, drawing a swift M on to her upper lip then smacking her lips together. 'It suits me too, didn't get a moment to fix my face. With all your shenanigans . . .'

Tulip and Ali looked at each other. It was completely possible that Nan-Nan was just going to bareface-and-lipstick her way out of this. But then they had one of their unspoken conversations, with Ali frowning, and Tulip tilting her head. Neither twin was really sure the mean hoarse-voiced bundle of rags could possibly have been their straight-talking, fast-rolling Nan.

'So, you got here fast,' said Tulip, carefully. 'Did you have time to change?'

'Why are you being weird, munchkin?' asked Mum, who had zero filters. 'Is it me, Mama, or are they both being weird?'

'I honestly can't tell any more, Minnie,' Nan-Nan said. 'They're your problem. You're mine. Circle of life.'

Mum was distracted, she'd seen a tall woman with an impressive fountain of red-ribboned braids stride past like royalty, with an entourage of scrubs scuttling behind her. 'The vascular team!' she said. 'They must be here for poor Momo, I'll go see him with them.'

'Momo?' said Nan-Nan. 'Is he here? In hospital?'

'Were you hoping he wasn't?' said Ali, raising an eyebrow. A bit inexpertly, as both eyebrows went up, so she just looked surprised.

'Watch the girls for me, Mama-bear, love you,' said Mum hurriedly, rushing after the troop of scrubs.

'Hey, Miss Glory,' she called, 'wait up, doncha wanna neuro opinion?'

'Get back in your brain-box, brainiac,' called

Miss Glory, the tall braided woman, over her shoulder. 'Last time I checked, the popliteal artery wasn't in the head.'

'For a plumber, you're pretty mouthy,' said Mum, racing after her.

'Consultant plumber to you,' snapped Miss Glory. 'Just 'cause you electricians don't like getting wet.'

Mum had reached her and did an exaggerated 'I'm-not-worthy' bow.

'C'mon, consultant. Your patient's my mate,' said Mum. 'Let me see him.'

'Fine,' said Miss Glory. 'I guess he'll need a software check.'

CHECK PAGE 299 OF THE APPENDIX FOR THE MINI-MEDIX BLOG POST

TWINTERMISSION! PLUMBERS AND ELECTRICIANS AKA VASCULAR SURGEONS AND NEUROSURGEONS AND WHY SURGEONS AREN'T CALLED DOCTOR!

Nan-Nan was looking at the twins with alarm. 'Girls?' she said, with an unusual quiver of fear in her voice. 'So is that REAL blood? It's not yours, is it?'

Either Nan-Nan was a great actress, or she really didn't know what had happened. The girls knew that both were possible. Tulip made a decision first.

'Oh Nan-Nan,' Tulip cried, running up to her and giving her a huge hug. 'It's Momo's blood! He had this horrible woman in his cab, and she got really cross when she saw us, and when she got out, we think she . . . she . . . stabbed him! With her cane. On purpose. And then she just hobbled off.'

She pulled back, realizing that she'd put blood all over Nan-Nan's jacket. 'Oh, I'm sorry.'

'Nonsense,' said Nan-Nan briskly. 'This is Pure Pleather. Plastic Leather for Leisure and Pleasure Pursuits. It's wipe clean for wet work.'

'Another old lady was doing the wet work today,' said Ali. 'Nan-Nan, the attacker was limping. And Momo said she was wearing a curly red wig. And she was all hidden in hideous clothes.'

'The *other* limpy old lady sounds just delightful,' said Nan-Nan, dryly. She pulled out her phone and wheeled off faster than they could follow. They ended up jogging after her.

'Come on, spit-spot,' Nan-Nan called over her shoulder.

'Where's she going?' complained Ali.

'I think she's a bit cross that you called her an old lady,' said Tulip.

'Some people are way too sensitive,' huffed Ali.

They found themselves in a bit of the hospital they hadn't been to before. It was weirdly quiet, and brightly coloured.

'Oh,' said Tulip, looking around at the boards, with timetables and topic teaching displayed in bright headings. 'It's the hospital school.'

'In you go,' said Nan-Nan. 'I need to do some digging, and this is the least suspicious place to leave a child.'

'A child? There's two of us,' said Ali, bristling at being called a child. 'Thought you could count.'

'Spit-spot,' said Nan-Nan, waving to the play therapist, and she wheeled away.

'Are you patient siblings?' said the play therapist, bustling over to them and looking at their red-stained clothes. 'Were you in Painting the Body art therapy? The fake blood's clever, isn't it? But we really should have given you some aprons.'

'Um, yeah,' said Ali. 'Art therapy.'

'Can we scrape some of this goo off, please?' added Tulip.

'Of course,' said the therapist. 'We've not got any more activities running for the day, so try the calming sensation room, once you've washed yourselves up. We've just changed the bulbs.'

The girls stood by the long sink, yanking off their blazers. Tulip scrubbed away Momo's blood. It ran down the sink in a pretty, pink trickle.

'Maybe you should have kept it as evidence,' said Ali. She pulled a plastic apron off the roll on the wall, and wrapped up her own blazer.

'You just can't be bothered to wash it,' said Tulip. But she said it kindly.

It felt like there was a lot to take in.

The end of term. The cancelled holiday. The mad bundle-of-rags woman. The pointy cane. The fountain of blood. Momo's blood.

It was all bustling for attention in Tulip's head. She was upset for Momo, and she was proud that they'd stopped him haemorrhaging, and she felt ashamed that she was still a bit upset about the holiday not happening.

'You know what,' said Tulip, 'I could do with some calming sensations.'

'I could do with some chocolate. But whatevs,' said Ali, following her out.

Tulip pushed open the door to the sensory room. It was dark, but rainbow colours were swirling around the walls of the room while gently wailing whale music played. There was a soothing voice talking through a beach-side meditation, saying things like, 'Feel the sand between your toes. To feel your feet, you must first touch the ground.'

'Lame!' sniggered Ali. 'Hey, I'm doing an interpretative dance, check me out.' She stuck out her arms at angles, and walked like a robot, right into a beanbag. She toppled over it and fell onto a small, prone body lying flat on its face.

'Aargh!' she screamed, leaping up. 'It's dead!'

'He's not dead,' said an offended voice from the next beanbag. The small body sat up, and yanked off a pair of headphones.

'Aargh! It's alive!' Ali screamed.

'You're saying that like it's a bad thing,' commented Tulip, groping along the wall. She found the light switch, and flicked it on. Sitting on the beanbags, blinking up at them in the sudden light, were Zac and Jay.

'What are you doing HERE?' Zac and Jay said. 'Jinx!' they said together. 'Jinx, padlock, 1-2-3!'

'Ha!' said Ali, rapidly recovering. 'You guys talk in creepy-twin unison too!'

'Jay-Jay-Jay, Zac-Zac-Zac,' said Tulip, kindly breaking the triple jinx. They'd recently decided it took three times to break the jinx, as it was too easy to break it by accident in school.

Jay pushed himself up from his beanbag with difficulty. It was squashy and had pretty much sucked his long legs into it. 'Yeah, it must be infectious.'

'Twinfectious,' grinned Zac, nudging Tulip.

'Aww,' said Tulip, laughing, 'totally twinfectious! You read my . . .'

'Yeah, yeah, he reads your blog,' said Jay, replacing his glasses. 'I only read it because of my concerns with data protection and patient confidentiality . . .'

Ali interrupted crossly, 'Don't think you're gonna distract us with your nerd nattering. We just caught you stalking us in the hospital.'

'Wow, someone thinks a lot of herself,' said Jay.

'Technically, you're stalking us,' said Zac. 'You walked in on us. We were meditating. Mum says it's good for . . .'

'You still haven't said why you're here,' persisted Ali.

Tulip kicked her. Not too subtle, she knew. But she was used to doing it to stop Ali saying something she might regret later. She'd just worked out why Zac and Jay were dumped in the children's school, after school hours.

'How's your mum?' she asked, quietly. 'Are you guys OK?'

The boys looked at each other, like they were deciding whether to tell. They had one of those silent conversations that the girls sometimes had. There was a head shake from Jay and a questioning look from Zac.

But Zac shrugged and said it anyway. 'Mum freaked when she heard what had happened to Momo. It was just too close to home. And she's not been well, you know, and it sort of tipped her over. It was like she couldn't breathe. She was getting all dizzy and tingly. And they brought her in here. And so Dad came. And then we had to come, just in case . . .'

'We're fine,' snapped Jay. 'We're basically baggage. It's just 'cause Dad couldn't find a babysitter at zero notice. We've never had one.'

'How's Momo?' asked Zac. 'Meant to text.'

'Wow,' said Tulip, 'your mum's poorly, and you're worried about the other guy. That's so nice.'

'Yeah,' said Zac, and he sounded a little bitter. 'Everyone says that. I'm the nicest kid in the world.'

He and Tulip looked at each other. It was like they both got what it meant. To be stuck being the nice one, because their twin had already bagsied the grumpy one, and got to act out whenever they felt like it.

Nan-Nan came rolling back. She didn't bat an eye when she saw the other twins. It was like she'd known they'd be there.

'Well,' she said to the girls. 'I think I'd better take you home.'

'Well what?' said Ali. 'What's the intel? You got on the case, right?'

Nan-Nan looked at her blankly. 'Intel? Case? I don't think I know what that means, dear.'

'Hi, Mrs Nan-Nan,' said Zac politely. 'How

are you?'

'Hello, Zac-or-Jay,' said Nan-Nan, who didn't know which was which and wasn't diplomatic enough to hide it. 'Call me Ruby. And don't call me Mrs. I never married. I made a particular point of it. I had a reputation for losing my boyfriends to hideous impending dooms.'

She suddenly grinned at the boys, with a nuclear flash of her bright white teeth, and they started laughing, like she'd made a joke.

'Heard that your mum's in for the night,' Nan-Nan said. 'Would you like to come back with the girls for a sleepover? I'll text your dad.'

'Oh, sure,' said Zac, looking at Jay for approval.

'Um, OK, I guess,' said Jay.

'NO!' said Ali, but she realized she'd shouted it out loud instead of saying it inside her head. 'Or something more sympathetic,' she added brightly.

As they walked away from the hospital school, Jay said to Ali and Tulip, in a slightly besotted voice, 'Your nan's amazing.'

'She's up to something,' hissed Ali to Tulip. 'Pretending not to have intel on the Momo case, inviting dumb-and-bummer back to ours so we can't quiz her . . .'

'They're our friends,' protested Tulip.

'I don't wanna share my room with them,' said Ali. 'It's bad enough that I have to share it with YOU.'

'And I've got some good news for you,' added Nan-Nan over her shoulder. 'The holiday's back on. Minnie still has to work over half term. So it'll just be you two, and me.'

'Really?' said Tulip, surprised. 'Yay! Where we going?'

'Oh just somewhere far, far away. For no particular reason,' said Nan-Nan airily. 'With no unusual or dangerous activity of any sort. No stabby-happy pensioners either.'

Tulip's delight began tingling into another feeling. Suspicion.

'You're right,' she whispered to Ali. 'She's up to something. She's getting us out the way! She knows that something's going down round here!'

'And we're gonna find out what,' said Ali. 'Double detectives on the case! What makes someone want to talk?'

'Filling the silence!' said Tulip. And she and Ali did a fist bump and pulled back with wavy fingers.

CHAPTER 3:
THE CAT GOES MWAH-HA-HA-HA

In the car, Ali and Tulip were quiet. Too quiet. Jay and Zac looked between the two of them in confusion.

'They're freaking me out,' Zac said in a stage whisper to Jay, who was sitting in the front seat, as he was the tallest by a whole hand. 'It's like we can say anything we want. I mean, I'm not used to even finishing a sentence around them.'

'Did we jinx them or something?' said Jay, equally confused.

'Don't think so,' said Zac. He spoke to the girls. 'Are you blanking us? Is this silent treatment? What've we done?'

'That's a bit egotistical,' commented Nan-Nan. 'I'm the grown-up here, it's more probably something to do with me.'

Tulip and Ali looked at each other meaningfully. This was the chance to get Nan-Nan to spill on what she'd found out about Momo.

'Why do you think it's to do with you, Nan-Nan?' enquired Tulip sweetly.

'What's the difference between ignorance and indifference?' said Nan-Nan.

'Don't know. Don't care,' said Ali. 'Duh.'

'Quite,' said Nan-Nan.

'Sometimes,' said Tulip carefully, to the car at large, 'we're quiet. Because we don't have anything we want to say.' She gave Ali a significant look. 'If other people want to say stuff, go ahead. Spill.'

'Oh, is this because you're annoyed that we're staying over?' said Jay. 'That's classic twins.'

'Oh puh-leeze,' huffed Ali. 'Conceited, much? It's not all about you.'

Nan-Nan pulled up outside their house and waved to their cat, who looked at her with supreme disdain, and slunk off into the shadows.

'Witchy's annoyed about something,' said Tulip to Nan-Nan. She noticed that Nan-Nan looked a bit shifty, like she knew why.

'She'll be less annoyed when it's time for leftovers,' said Nan-Nan brightly. 'I'm making *moules marinières* for dinner.'

'Do you know what that means?' asked Jay.

'Don't know, don't care,' said Ali.

Ali and Tulip went upstairs, dragged out the fold-out sofa in their room and dumped a couple of sleeping bags on it.

'Bed's made,' announced Tulip.

'Wow,' said Zac, 'that was efficient.'

'We used to do the sleepover thing a lot,' said Ali. 'In other people's houses, though. 'Cause mum was always working.'

'Yeah,' said Tulip, 'we stopped when we realized we were never gonna be able to invite people back over.'

'We're the other way,' said Zac. 'We've had loads of sleepovers at ours. But Mum never lets us stay over at someone else's. She gets too worried.'

'Huh,' said Jay. 'So that's . . . nice, I guess. We

get to have a sleepover out, and you get to have a sleepover in.'

'Weird that someone had to end up in the hospital for that to happen,' commented Ali.

Tulip looked at her sharply. But then she realized that Ali wasn't being sarcastic for once. She was just being honest. She looked a little sad, even. Ali saw that Tulip was looking at her, and gave her the Don't-Pity-Me face and stuck her tongue out.

Zac fluffed up the sleeping bags on the mattress, and began picking up the stuff around the bed, and folding the girls' clothes into neat triangles.

'What are you doing?' snapped Ali.

'It's his nervous habit,' said Jay. 'He tidies when he's uncomfortable.'

'You don't have to *he* me,' complained Zac. 'I'm right here.' He pulled open a drawer. 'There's loads of room here,' he commented, slotting the clothes in.

'That's because our clothes are all on the floor, duh,' said Ali.

'It's easier to see them that way,' said Tulip apologetically.

'You can see them like this,' said Zac, pointing

at the triangles. 'Look, I folded them upright.'

'You're gonna make someone a great little house-elf one day,' said Jay.

'He's just jealous because Mum says I'm better at this stuff than him,' shrugged Zac.

'Yeah, hit me where it hurts,' scoffed Jay. 'My housework skills.'

'If I do it, Mum doesn't have to,' said Zac simply.

Tulip and Ali looked at each other. Sometimes Zac's shining niceness made them feel a bit ashamed. Jay just looked cross, like his brother had shown him up, again.

'Folding looks fun,' said Tulip, supportively.

'Not as fun as this,' said Ali, leaping into the pile of clothes and snow-angelling on them.

'You could seriously hide a body under this pile of rags,' said Jay, picking up a T-shirt and holding it at arm's length. 'And this stuff isn't clean. What's that? Ketchup? Mustard? Mould?'

'Camouflage,' said Tulip.

'You could hide ANYBODY under a pile of rags with some camouflage,' mused Ali. She looked at Tulip, as something struck her.

Tulip nodded, like she'd got there too. 'You mean the old-lady-assassin from the cab. She really could have been *anyone*.'

'Like any old lady?' asked Zac, confused.

'Any guy or girl at all,' said Ali, impatiently. She threw a pile of clothes over Jay.

'Argh, stop it!' he complained.

'I'm making a point,' said Ali, shoving the bowler hat from her Victorian Day costume on his head, and draping the scarf from Egyptian Day over it with a couple of beanie-boos over the brim. She rammed a pair of oversized sunglasses onto his face.

'See,' she said triumphantly.

'I can't see,' muttered Jay. 'Not sure I want to.'

'I'm not sure narrowing it down to ANYONE is that helpful, though,' mused Tulip. 'Maybe she really WAS an old lady, and wanted us to think she wasn't. Double bluff.'

Jay was shaking off the costume. 'Can't believe you made me a dress-shop dummy in your crime scene reconstruction,' he complained. 'Non-organic cotton makes me itch.'

Ali rolled her eyes at him. 'Our room, our rules,' she said, opening the door. 'Feel free to go downstairs.' She wrinkled her nose, as a pungent fishy waft floated into the room.

'What's your nan making for supper?' asked Zac. 'Does she know we're gluten-free veggies?'

'Preferably organic,' added Jay.

'Yep, it's written on the note on your back next to Kick Me,' said Ali cheerfully.

'It smells like she's boiling up seawater,' said Zac, looking like a frowny-face emoji.

'Maybe she is. She's doing a RECIPE with a funny French name,' sighed Tulip. 'She's always doing recipes.'

'You'll get used to it,' agreed Ali. 'If you stick around long enough.'

'Aww, really?' said Jay, surprised.

'Hey, that wasn't an invitation,' snapped Ali. 'If I want a four-eyed geek in the house I'll just . . .'

'Put on a pair of Harry Potter novelty specs and look in the mirror?' suggested Tulip, sweetly.

'I was gonna say advertise,' said Ali, 'but respect. Your idea didn't suck.'

She reached out and plucked off Jay's specs, and put them on. 'Hey, these look way better on me than they do on you,' she crowed. 'It's not the specs that are nerdy, it's you!'

'Give those back,' complained Jay. 'I'll stumble over all the rubbish in this pit.'

'Great, have a nice *trip*,' crowed Ali.

'Ali! You're being mean,' said Tulip reproachfully. 'They're our guests.'

'Yeah, give them back,' said Zac. His arms were full of paper for recycling that he'd collected from around the room.

'Sure. What's the magic word?' said Ali to Jay.

'Now!' roared Jay. 'Or I'll mess up your room.'

'Good luck with that,' said Ali. 'You'll probably just accidentally put something back in its place.' She waved to herself in the mirror, 'Bye-bye, super-smart-speccy Ali,' and she pulled them off and threw his glasses over to him. He caught them clumsily at his chest.

'Bye-bye, Superman; Hello, Clark Kent,' Jay said, smugly, as he put them back on.

'It's like you think Clark Kent is better,' commented Ali.

'He's so much better,' said Zac. 'He's an award-winning journalist who has a useful job and doesn't wear his pants on the outside.'

'Not a flamboyant vigilante in primary colours with high-maintenance-man-curls,' agreed Tulip.

Suddenly they heard Nan-Nan's voice

crackling from the walls, 'Hey, don't knock flamboyant vigilantes, we get the job done.'

'Nan-Nan?' asked Tulip, looking around. 'How did you get up the stairs?'

'I installed some new tech,' said Nan-Nan. 'Got bored of yelling up the stairs like some eighties sitcom. In a civilized country, no woman should have to shout to be heard.'

'Think Ali's declared our room its own country,' commented Tulip. 'Deffo not a civilized one. Shouting is where she *starts* on the noise ladder.'

'Goes up through to Pirate Bellow and then full Banshee Shriek,' agreed Ali, proudly. 'I once broke glass.'

Nan-Nan laughed, 'Come on down, supper's up. It's . . .'

'A *recipe*,' said Ali gloomily, heading down the stairs. 'Don't get your hopes up, boys.'

Downstairs, Ali and Tulip were looking on with furious bewilderment, as Zac and Jay hoovered up their dinner, and put their hands up for seconds.

'This is totally unfair,' said Tulip, looking sadly down at the mussel shells swimming in briny sauce with green bits of parsley scattered over them like wilted grass clippings. 'How come we get boiled exoskeleton, and they get a TAKEAWAY?'

'Well, they're veggie, darlings,' said Nan-Nan. 'And food is about experimentation. The boys have never had an Indian takeaway.'

'We've had home-made organic chickpea curry,' said Zac, 'but it was nothing like this! I've never had food that came in a BOX before . . .'

'Whoever invented these is a genius,' said Jay, showing them the foil cartons. 'Look, you can eat STRAIGHT OUT OF THEM! No washing up!'

'Joke's on you,' said Ali. 'We pretty much eat takeout all the time when Nan-Nan's not around. We get BORED of takeout.'

'She's lying,' said Tulip.

'I know,' said Jay. 'Who could ever get bored of THIS!' and he pulled a crispy poori from a paper bag and dipped it lingeringly in the spicy sauce.

'I'll swap you,' said Ali, urgently, under her breath.

'Hard pass,' said Jay. 'I'm vegetarian. Can't

eat your mussels. Though they smell SOOO delicious, Nan-Nan Ruby.'

'Hard pass, too,' said Zac, when Ali stared hard at him instead. 'I'm not sure those things are even dead.'

'They were alive when I bought them,' agreed Nan-Nan. 'They have to be, so they open in the heat of the pot. That's how mussels work.' She was dipping her baguette into her mussels, and eating them with relish. 'Yum. I might do carpaccio next. That's raw meat, but it's sliced thin,' she added helpfully to the boys.

'Never mind your weird world food experiments,' said Ali, pushing away her mussels, in case they woke up and decided to attack her. 'Just tell us what you found out about Momo.'

'Yeah, you must have found out something,' said Tulip. 'You dumped us in the hospital school for a reason. And THEN you said you were taking us away. Like it's not safe here.'

'Other way around,' commented Jay. 'Least safe place to be is usually wherever you guys are.'

'He's still annoyed you attacked him with your laundry and dressed him like an old lady,' said Zac in a stage whisper.

Jay glared at him.

'I don't know anything about poor Momo,' insisted Nan-Nan. 'Just that some old lady hobbled out of Momo's cab, did a subtle bit of slashing, and then disappeared down the street. And she was wrapped up in layers like a mummy in the Primark bargain bucket.'

'Aha!' said Ali. 'We knew that. But how did you?'

'We told her,' Tulip reminded her.

'We told her, too,' said Zac, his mouth stuffed with samosa. 'They've put peas and peppers in this. It's like our school snack box nuked with fried pastry!'

'Is that a good thing?' asked Tulip.

'Such a good thing,' confirmed Zac.

'So the attacker had a LIMP,' said Ali, looking meaningfully at Nan-Nan's wheelchair. 'And a ginger wig.'

'Yep,' said Nan-Nan, not batting an eyelid. 'You told me that, too. Why are you being weird?'

'It's just that the red curly wig is *your* go-to costume for your super-spy act!' said Ali. 'Why is an attacker dressing like you, limping like you? There's gotta be a link!'

'The only other person who knew about your

secret identity is swimming down the Thames,'
added Tulip, brainstorming furiously. 'Did you
tell someone else about your ginger persona?
Maybe you KNOW Momo's attacker!'

Nan-Nan's face actually blazed with fury.
'Flattered that's what you think I'm capable of,
girls,' she said quietly. 'You think I collude with
stabby criminals? I think I need a moment. Give
your food to the cat. At least she'll appreciate it.'

'Oh, Nan-Nan,' said Tulip, realizing they'd
gone too far. Nan-Nan looked really upset. It
was strange not to have her laughing at them
with a funny put-down.

'There's gluten-free trifle in the fridge,' said
Nan-Nan stiffly. 'Children who don't think I'm
capable of conspiring in attempted murder can
have some.' She wheeled out of the room.

'Did she say gluten-free trifle?' Jay raised his
head from his samosa. 'That's like my favourite
word combination ever! Your nan's awesome.'

'Read the room, dude,' said Zac, looking at Ali
and Tulip, who had the look on their faces that
Snape must've had when Dumbledore told him
he could've been in Gryffindor. Like it wasn't
their fault they were horrible people.

'You're not horrible people,' he said to them

kindly. 'I'm sure lots of people accuse their grans of criminal associations.'

'Stop mind-reading, freak-geek,' snapped Ali.

'It's not our fault,' said Tulip. 'She's so Nan-Nan all the time, it's hard to tell what's going on.'

She and Ali took their plates of mussel shells to the front door, and left them outside for Witch and her gangland feline friends. They had been hanging around smugly on the wall like the big kids who smoked outside the school gates in posing packs. Witch leapt on the bowl first, and turned her tail on them, hissing at her friends to show who was boss.

'So now she's the alpha cat?' said Ali. 'I think power's gone to her head.'

'Yeah, and a thank you would be nice,' said Tulip.

'You should've got a dog,' said Ali. 'Dogs are pathetically grateful.'

'Come on,' Tulip said, 'let's good cop and bad cop the Bat-Nan.'

'Who gets to be bad cop?' said Ali, and then whooped, 'Psych! Like it's ever a choice. Hahaha.'

'You're such a noob,' said Tulip. 'I'm only good cop because you could never get away with it. It's like it's not even in your vocabulary.'

'Least I can spell vocabulary,' pointed out Ali.

They went into the sitting room. Nan-Nan had her back to them and was staring at the blank grey fuzz of the TV, which was switched on, but with no signal. She was lit by the cold shimmering glare, and her wheelchair glinted menacingly, as did the studs of her leather jacket.

'You gotta give it to her, she knows how to set a mood,' whispered Ali.

'Nan-Nan,' said Good-Cop-Tulip gently. 'What really happened to Momo? And why are you taking us away? And where? You do know something, don't you?'

'Girls,' said Nan-Nan stiffly. 'I've been expecting you.'

'Duh, we live here,' said Bad-Cop-Ali. 'Why didn't you get a cat to stroke, while you were at it?'

Nan-Nan's wheelchair turned around. They saw that she WAS stroking a cat. Black, like Witch. But with dead, metallic eyes.

'Meet the new housekeeper,' she said. 'We're going to need someone here to keep up appearances. Your damn cat has to come with us.'

Witch appeared at the window, hissed furiously

at the fake cat on Nan-Nan's lap, and scratched the glass.

'Oh,' said Tulip. 'That's why Witch's upset. You've brought another cat in on her territory.'

'But where are we gonna be?' said Ali. 'You're not really just taking us on holiday?'

'Not a holiday. We're going to a hotel,' confirmed Nan-Nan.

'Nice,' said Ali, sincerely. 'About time.'

But Nan-Nan's face darkened. 'The opposite of nice! It's a HORRIBLE CAT-ASTROPHE of a hotel!'

The cat let out a robotic *Mwah-ha-ha-ha*!

The girls looked at each other in horror.

'That spiralled out pretty fast,' whispered Ali.

'Why would we want to go to a horrible hotel . . .' started Tulip.

'Where did you get the Metal-Meow . . .' Ali talked over her.

'No follow-up questions,' snapped Nan-Nan. 'Go! We leave at dawn!'

The girls trudged up the stairs, defeated.

'And you guys say that I'm the one with the flair for the dramatic,' muttered Ali.

CHAPTER 4:
BiN-DiViNG

Ali and Tulip were in bed when their mum finally came home. The boys were fast asleep on the sofa-bed mattress on the floor. Ali could hear them snuffling contentedly. She could hear Mum doing her usual squealing with delight that Nan-Nan had loaded the dishwasher for her and probably laid out hot food and trifle.

'Tulip,' hissed Ali, 'you awake?'

'Nope,' said Tulip, snuffling deeper into her pillow.

'Nan-Nan'll be leaving in a bit,' said Ali.

'Yup,' said Tulip.

'You're rubbish conversation when you're asleep,' complained Ali.

Tulip replied with a snort that turned into a snore.

'OK, Sleeping-Snooty, I'm going on duty,' said Ali, and she flicked on the fairy lights that were knotted around her bed. The room was lit in grisly green and orange, as the tangle of lights were from last Halloween, and the girls had never tried to untie them. Grinning skulls and leering pumpkin-heads beamed at them with brittle menace.

'TMI,' yawned Tulip. 'Don't flush, you'll wake the boys.'

'What?' said Ali. 'I said on *duty*. I'm gonna tail Nan-Nan.'

'What!' echoed Tulip, waking up properly. 'No, you're not. She's cross with us. She got cross enough to download a *Mwah-ha-ha* to the robot cat.'

'So she can't get any crosser,' said Ali, illogically.

'She's coming back AT DAWN,' pointed out Tulip. 'What's she gonna do between then and now?'

'I DON'T KNOW!' complained Ali. 'That's

the point of following her. If I knew what she was gonna do, I wouldn't have to, duh!'

'Shh, the little ones are sleeping,' said Tulip, peering over the side of her bed. The boys were snuggled up together in their sleeping bags like kittens.

'Aww,' she said, 'look at them! I think they're holding hands. That's so sweet.'

'Don't get ideas,' said Ali. 'If I wake up and find you pawing me like a puppy, I'll karate chop your neck.'

'And you wonder why I get all the cuddles,' said Tulip. 'Why aren't they waking up?'

'They're normally in bed at seven thirty,' scoffed Ali. 'Think we kept them up about two hours past their bedtime.'

'Must be nice, not to be woken up by someone hissing random schemes at them,' said Tulip.

'Stop staring at them while they're asleep, it's creepy,' said Ali. 'You coming or what?'

'What,' said Tulip, firmly.

'Haha, funny,' said Ali. She got out of bed and stumbled over the Lego shrapnel and piles of fluffy guff all over the floor. Zac had cleared a lot of the clothes mountain, but there was still a mixed mulch of Tulip's stuffed toys and Iron

Man helmets.

Tulip spotted that Ali was already double-dressed in her traditional two T-shirts, a short-sleeved one over a long-sleeved one, and wearing leggings, with shorts on top. This didn't surprise Tulip. Ali often went to bed fully dressed to save time in the morning. She'd been known to hide breakfast in her bed, too. Usually bowls of dry cereal. She tried putting scrambled eggs there, once, but it hadn't worked out well.

'Come ON,' said Ali, at the door.

Tulip sighed and heaved herself out of bed. 'I'm not following you,' she insisted. 'I'm just looking out for you. As usual.'

She carefully picked her way past the boys' snoring bodies, and crept down the stairs in her bare feet. Nan-Nan and Mum were still chatting in the kitchen. She could hear their mum happily munching and yakking between mouthfuls.

'Momo'll be alright, Mama,' she was saying. 'What MONSTER could have done that to him? He's like the loveliest kid alive. He was literally helping old ladies and children.'

'Doubt it was anything to do with Momo,' said Nan-Nan, briskly. 'More likely the people he knows.'

'I suppose cabbies hear lots of secrets,' mused Mum. 'Wonder who could have got him in trouble.'

'No idea. So I'll be scooting off, Minnie,' said Nan-Nan. A bit too briskly. 'Remember, the boys are organic gluten-free sugar-free veggies.'

'Oh Mama-bear, that's a bit uncalled for,' said Mum.

'Amazingly, not a joke,' said Nan-Nan.

They could hear Nan-Nan wheeling around on her manual setting.

'Quick!' said Ali, pushing her feet into her trainers. 'She's coming.'

Tulip sighed and grabbed her plastic wellies, which were the closest shoes to the door.

They carefully opened the door, and shut it with a gentle click. And then hopped over the neighbour's low wall, and crouched there. Tulip pulled on her boots.

'End of term, they said. Have a great break, they said,' she muttered. 'And I'm on my butt on a wet lawn at midnight.'

Ali's eyes were sparkling. 'Ah, you know you love the drama,' she said.

'Nope, you love the drama, and I'm the one stuck LOOKING AFTER you,' hissed Tulip.

'Why don't I do something stupid so you can look after me, for a change?'

'Aw, don't beat yourself up,' said Ali. 'Every superhero needs a sidekick.'

'What!' said Tulip.

'And every comedian needs a straight dude,' Ali added.

'Sidekick?' blustered Tulip. 'Straight dude?' She got up. 'That's it, funny girl, I'm out. Hard pass on the Ali-antics tonight. I'm switching OFF the Ali-Show.'

But then Nan-Nan opened the door, still chatting to Mum, and Ali grabbed at Tulip's pyjamas, so she had to crouch down again.

'In a while, crocodile,' they heard Nan-Nan call back to Mum. And then she was wheeling down the street. She didn't get in her car.

'Huh,' said Tulip. She'd sort of assumed they'd hop in the back while Nan-Nan was sorting out her wheelchair. And that Nan-Nan would spot them, because they weren't exactly twin ninjas, and would tell them off, and send them back to bed, and that would be the end of that.

'C'mon,' said Ali, and she followed Nan-Nan in the shadows.

'Can't believe we're doing this, we're tailing

our own Nan-Nan,' Tulip muttered. 'It's sick.'

'Sooo sick,' said Ali, excitedly, like it was the best thing ever.

'Someone should really decide what that word means,' complained Tulip.

Nan-Nan was wheeling doggedly down the road, still on her manual setting, so there was no motorized hum. She sailed almost silently through the shadows. The girls kept low, avoiding the pools of amber light thrown by the streetlamps, sticking to the low walls of the neighbours' front gardens.

Nan-Nan stopped at the stain where Momo's blood had sunk into the speckled stone of the pavement. She shone a light from her phone, pulled out a claw-stick and plucked something from the ground, popping it into a little plastic bag.

'Shouldn't there be a tape or something around that stain?' hissed Ali. 'She's mopping up the evidence.'

'Kids who get stabbed must be a priority,' said Tulip. 'Guessing the police have probably already got all the evidence they want.'

'Stabbed kids a priority?' said Ali. 'Wow, you're naïve.'

'Like you can even spell naïve,' snapped Tulip.

Nan-Nan's head jerked up suddenly, like a meerkat on high alert, and turned around. A black cat hissed and leapt off the wall, a few steps behind her.

'Good kitty,' said Nan-Nan out loud. 'Keep an eye out for me.'

She carried on around the corner, in the direction that the wrapped-up woman had hobbled off. The girls went to follow, but the cat started purring.

'Shush, Witchy,' whispered Tulip, reaching to stroke her thick, black fur. But before she even touched her, she knew something was wrong. She didn't feel any heat coming from the cat.

The cat turned its head. Slowly and smoothly. Like a train on a track. And then one of the eyes flashed like it had taken a picture.

'Don't think that's Witch,' said Ali.

Tulip was going to point out that she'd got that already, but then the robot Witch let out a *Mwah-ha-ha*. Top volume. They both jumped.

'I'm gonna smash that stupid cog-pile into paperclips,' hissed Ali.

'I wouldn't,' said Nan-Nan. She was wheeling back around the corner, looking with amusement at a picture on her phone. She showed it to them. It was the gaping, gormless shot that the Robo-Cat had just taken. Their eyes were half-closed and their mouths were half-open.

'You girls are not photogenic,' she grinned. 'And Twitch was just doing her job. Tailing you. Security detail.'

Ali gave Robo-Cat a death stare, which was completely wasted on the robot, although it flashed and sent another pic to Nan-Nan's phone.

'Yikes,' said Nan-Nan, checking out the shot. 'Ali's you're-dead-to-me face should come with some sort of health warning.'

'So,' said Tulip, trotting up to Nan-Nan in her plastic boots, 'the cat's tailing us, we're tailing you . . . so who are YOU tailing?'

'Good question,' grinned Nan-Nan.

Tulip stared back at Ali, and then at Nan-Nan. They were both thinking that 'Good question' wasn't much of an answer, and was something grown-ups said when they didn't want to tell you stuff.

'What are you even doing out here?' blurted out Ali, crossly. 'Contaminating the crime scene?'

'An even better question,' said Nan-Nan, her smile becoming wider. 'When did you become so forensically minded?'

'You're looking for clues!' said Tulip. 'It's about Momo's attacker! You're gonna track her down!'

'Let's not get ahead of ourselves,' said Nan-Nan. 'But it's worth checking out where she . . . or he . . . went. There was nothing in Momo's car we could use, no fingerprints, not even a natural hair . . .'

'So that's why she was covered in so many clothes like a mad bag lady,' said Ali. 'She was hiding something! She'd PLANNED to do something . . .'

'And my tech-minded gal-pals in the lab didn't find any CCTV,' said Nan-Nan. 'This suburban hell you live in has nothing, the closest camera covers the bus stop, and she didn't get on a bus.'

'Come on,' said Tulip, walking around the corner, 'let's check it out, anyway.'

Ali and Nan-Nan followed Tulip, as she lit her mobile, and swept it in an arc in front of her. There was a bin overflowing with Friday fish wrappers, set back from the road, just before the bus stop.

'Hold on,' said Ali, 'whadya doing?'

She watched in disgust as Tulip got a big stick and shoved it in the bin.

'Just checking something out,' said Tulip.

'Gross, that's not how you go fishing,' said Ali, as Tulip pulled out a large piece of half-eaten cod.

'I'm a bit offended that she's bin-diving for food,' commented Nan-Nan. 'The *moules* weren't that bad, were they?'

'There's no polite way to answer that,' said Tulip sweetly, 'so I'd rather not.'

She dropped the fish on the pavement, and the real Witch came scampering down the road, and began tearing into it.

'Seriously,' muttered Ali, 'that fat cat can smell out food within a mile radius.'

'Quit fat-shaming Witchy,' said Tulip. 'She's squishy and adorable.'

Witch hissed. She had caught sight of Twitch, and turned on her with immediate dislike and furry fury, clawing at her viciously.

'Yup, adorable,' agreed Nan-Nan.

Twitch just turned her head round 180 degrees and ignored Witch, who seemed to take this as some kind of victory, and carried on eating her fish.

'Ooh, I think I've got something,' said Tulip. 'It's under a lot of gunk.'

Witch leapt into the bin, scattering more fish bits out onto the street. She'd woken up the pigeons who were flocking down to eat the rancid leftovers.

'You know that littering's an eighty quid fine,' said Ali. 'Jay told me that, when I chucked my crisps at his head.'

'Well, I'm sure he deserved it,' sighed Tulip. 'What was he doing, correcting your grammar?'

'He held the door for me,' spat out Ali. 'Like I couldn't hold it for myself. He had it coming to him.'

Nan-Nan had caught sight of something glinting in the rubbish. 'Great work, Tulip,' she said suddenly, reaching out with the claw hand. 'We've got it!'

Ali went to have a look at it. 'Yeuch,' she said, 'it's like some old razor covered in ketchup.' Nan-Nan handed her a bag and gloves, and she dropped it in. 'Why is the end stuck in a bit of wood?'

'The cane! Check it out,' said Tulip triumphantly, fishing out something else. At the end of her stick, was a rolled-up pile of clothes, with a snapped walking stick.

'Everything but the wig,' said Ali. She was looking at the razor, fascinated and disgusted. 'This is the thing that got Momo? The thing that opened up his artery? But it's so small.'

'Small things can be deadly,' said Nan-Nan. 'Look at bacteria. Look at you two.' She grinned, and said, 'Great work, girls. I'm gonna get this back to the lab, and you two are heading home.'

At their door, the girls watched Nan-Nan get into her Nan-mobile.

'Don't worry, girls,' said Nan-Nan. 'We're going to find out who did this to Momo. Together. Their cabbie-stabby days are over.'

'You gonna tell us more about the horrible hotel?' asked Tulip.

'Don't push your luck,' grinned Nan-Nan. 'You'll find out tomorrow. It's the PURR-FECT place to do some investigating, though.'

They waved her off.

'PERFECT!' squeaked Tulip excitedly. 'We're going away AND we're gonna solve the case.'

'And you were suspicious of Nan-Nan!' scoffed Ali. 'Haha, you noob!'

Tulip was briefly annoyed at the unfairness of

this. 'You were! You're suspicious of everyone. You'd be suspicious of me if you weren't always on my back. You watch way too much telly.'

'You don't watch enough,' said Ali. 'That's why you don't know what anyone's talking about at school.'

They let themselves quietly into the house.

'You know what, though,' said Tulip quietly. 'We never found the red wig.'

CHAPTER 5:
PANCAKES AND PURR-FECT PLACES

The girls woke up to the sound of screaming. It wasn't coming from them, it was coming from the boys on the floor.

'Seriously, night terrors?' grumbled Ali. 'How old are you?'

'They're the same age as you, duh,' mumbled Tulip. 'Dudes, we're trying to sleep.'

The boys were looking around in horror, at the luminous, maniacally grinning skeleton and pumpkin heads. One was hanging right over the sofa bed, which could admittedly be a bit of a creepy thing to come face to face with when you'd just opened your eyes. The girls had forgotten to switch off the fairy-scary lights when they'd stumbled into bed.

'What's wrong with you people?' screeched Jay. 'Who *Halloweens* their room during the summer half term?'

'Chillax,' said Ali, 'they were left over from last Halloween.'

'Yeah, it's totes not malicious,' said Tulip, in a soothing tone. 'Just laziness.'

'I dunno,' grinned Ali, 'I like to think it's a little bit of both.'

'Switch-them-off,' whispered Zac. 'And-get-the-lights, I need my asthma inhaler.'

'I'll get it, little bro,' said Jay, leaping into action, and then he fell over a rancid pile of stinking stuff spilling out of a black bin bag.

'What's wrong with you?' he screeched again. 'You literally left TRASH next to the bed. Stinking, fetid TRASH!'

'It's evidence,' said Ali, promptly. 'We picked it up last night. Thought we could go through it together.'

'You went out late to pick up rubbish?' asked Zac, bleary-eyed, sucking on his inhaler. 'Didn't expect that kind of civic duty from you.'

'Enough with the civic duty, dweeb,' said Ali, bossily. 'Let's CSI the rubbish.'

'Hard pass,' said Jay. 'You guys have NO idea what a Sunny Saturday activity should be about.'

'Ooh, hey, it's Saturday!' squealed Tulip. 'That means Mum's here for breakfast!' She leapt out of bed and ran up the stairs. Mum was there, in the top room, surrounded by her clutter, snuffling gently into her pillow.

'Mama-bear!' yelped Tulip, bouncing on her.

'What! Where? No!' yelped Mum, leaping up, and hiding the plate of chocolate biscuits next to her bed under her duvet. She looked around. 'Oh, I thought you said Nan-Nan was here, munchkin,' she said, settling back down. 'You know, MY Mama-bear.'

'Why are you worried about seeing Nan-Nan?' said Tulip, cuddling up to Mum.

'Love her to bits, but she's a bit critical,' said Mum. 'She'll start on my hair . . .'

'Which is flooffy and adorable,' said Tulip, patting Mum's short fluff of hair which was sticking straight out in all directions.

'Then my outfit . . .'

'But everything you wear looks like pyjamas

or scrubs, even when it's not pyjamas or scrubs. It's like the most comfortable clothing combination ever . . .' said Tulip.

'Then my cholesterol and glucose . . .' Mum reached contentedly for a biscuit.

'Chocolate and sugar are like two of your five a day,' insisted Tulip. 'Nan-Nan's just jealous because she hasn't got enough squidge to survive as long as you on a desert island.'

'And then she'll tell me off, 'cause I'm working today,' finished Mum, sheepishly.

'You're what?' roared Ali, who had been standing at the top of the stairs. She'd been watching Tulip hugging Mum a bit jealously, holding back, as she hated looking needy, even though she liked cuddles just as much as Tulip. But getting cross about Mum's working hours was something she didn't have to hold back on.

'HOW DARE YOU?' Ali screamed. 'You've cancelled the holiday, and now you're cancelling the weekend too!'

'But Nan-Nan said you were heading off with her today, anyway,' said Mum, sensibly. Ali was annoyed as this made perfect sense. 'And they needed a hand at work. And we've got bills to pay.'

'Well if they're Bill's, he should pay them,' said Tulip. Ali rolled her eyes at her. 'What?' she said. 'Just trying to lighten the mood.'

'Cuddle?' said Mum, apologetically, lifting up the duvet.

'Humph,' said Ali, jumping in. 'This changes NOTHING. I'm still cross. It's always WORK, WORK, WORK with you. And Nan-Nan's right, you're a big fluff-headed ball of pre-diabetes who lives in pyjamas.'

'Love you, too, munchkin,' said Mum. She wrinkled her nose, 'What smells so bad?'

'That would be us,' said Tulip, helpfully. 'We were dumpster-diving.'

'And Nan-Nan's leftovers,' added Ali, squashing in on Mum's other side.

A clattering started happening in the kitchen, and then a delicious smell began wafting up the stairs. Mum, Ali, and Tulip looked at each other, and floated down after it, following their noses. Nan-Nan was in the kitchen, making pancakes with Jay and Zac.

'Oh, Mama-bear,' said Mum joyfully. 'You came back to make pancakes! That's my favourite!'

'Your second favourite,' said Nan-Nan. 'And don't get too excited, thanks to the picky princesses here, they're gluten-free, dairy-free and egg-free.'

'But not fun-free,' said Zac, flipping one excitedly.

'Oh yay,' said Tulip, insincerely, looking apologetically at Mum.

'You ruined pancakes!' complained Ali. 'I hate you. I hate you all.'

'So that's why I got your *favourite* favourite,' said Nan-Nan, tossing over a brown paper bag.

'Doughnuts!' squealed Mum and Tulip.

'Gimme that,' said Ali, grabbing the bag, and sitting at the table. She stuffed one in her face. 'I love you,' she said blissfully. 'I love you all.'

'So, here's the plan,' said Mum, pouring herself a coffee. 'I'll take the boys to the hospital so their dad can pick them up.' She smiled at Zac and Jay. 'He called last night. Wiggie said your mum's doing great.'

'Yay!' said Jay, grinning with relief. 'Celebratory pancake, Mrs Minnie?'

'Oh, no-no-no, more for you,' said Mum, hastily. 'And you'll have the girls, Mama,' she carried on. 'I'm sorry I took the extra shifts, but this stupid house is haemorrhaging money, all the repairs since poor insane Sprotland was here smashing stuff up, and I needed to check on Momo, anyway. His foster parents are coming up, too. They really wanted me there.'

'Don't worry about me and the girls. We'll have a lovely few days away,' said Nan-Nan. 'It's all been arranged. It's the PURR-FECT spot.'

Ali and Tulip both noticed Nan-Nan's weird emphasis on perfect. Extra-weird, as she'd made a point of telling them the hotel was horrible.

'Is she lying to us or to Mum?' asked Ali conversationally.

'I guess it could be horribly perfect, or perfectly horrible,' said Tulip.

Nan-Nan frowned at them, as they weren't being even slightly discreet, and distracted Mum by passing her another doughnut, with chocolate sprinkles and a fake flake.

'Oh, we can't afford a perfect hotel,' said Mum, happily accepting the doughnut. 'The one I'd booked in France just had character.'

'Character is hotel code for bedbugs,' said Nan-Nan. 'Think the girls had a lucky escape. Don't worry about the cash, my SWAT team are covering it. I won the sweepstake raffle thing.'

Ali and Tulip suddenly jerked up their heads, still chewing the chocolate centres of the doughnuts.

'Hey, did you spot that?' said Jay casually to Zac. 'Meerkat alert! They did that in creepy-twin sync.'

'SWAT team?' repeated Tulip. 'The Senior Water Aerobics Training team? The ladies you train with on Wednesday nights?'

'It's nice that senior citizens pull together like that,' said Mum. 'Thanks for breakfast, Mama-bear.'

Mum had no idea that Nan-Nan's mysterious SWAT team were nothing to do with old lady water aerobics on Wednesdays, and quite a lot to do with Nan-Nan's old job as a 'nanny'. An international, tech-tastic, super-spy nanny. When she cleared up a toxic mess, she wasn't talking about the girls' room. The girls had never been allowed to meet the SWAT team; once when Ali and Tulip accidentally crashed a training night, Nan-Nan had literally helter-skeltered them away, down a spiral ramp to her Bat-Nan basement.

After breakfast, Tulip and Ali waved off Mum and the boys, and impatiently waited for them to turn the corner, before running back to Nan-Nan in the kitchen.

'Where are we really going?' asked Ali, hopping with excitement. 'This is a SWAT mission! We're not really going to some lame bed and breakfast with a pool and a playground?'

'I think that a pool and a playground sounds quite nice,' commented Tulip. She petted Witch, who had leapt on the table, and sniffed the leftover pancakes, before turning away disdainfully.

'Just got some intel to gather,' said Nan-Nan, shoving Witch off the table. Witch slid into Mum's chair like she was the boss, purring smugly. 'We're going undercover.'

'Ooh, do we get to wear hats and BIG wigs and mean-mad-moustaches?' said Ali.

'I don't think you know what undercover means,' said Nan-Nan. 'It's about *not* being noticed. Just grab your toothbrushes and some underwear and your beddy-teddies. Don't bother about clothes, I'm going to get you something different from your usual costumes. You're a bit too noticeable as you are.'

'We just wear shorts and shirts and leggings,' protested Tulip.

'You're the one in the costume, Bat-Nan,'

scoffed Ali, flicking at Nan-Nan's leather jacket.

'But you're the ones who posed for the papers after stopping Sprotland, not me,' said Nan-Nan, wheeling herself to the front door. Her nose wrinkled, and she looked up the stairs. 'What smells so bad?' she asked.

'Everyone's asking that,' commented Ali. 'It's just the trash from the bin.'

'Excellent initiative,' grinned Nan-Nan. 'Baggie it up, we'll take it with us!'

'To prank your enemies?' suggested Ali, helpfully.

'Great,' complained Tulip. 'That's our big exciting holiday? A road trip with a bag of trash as a ride-along. The boys are right, we need to re-think our Sunny Saturday activities.'

'What's up with Thing 2?' asked Nan-Nan.

'Think she's cranky because she didn't get enough sleep,' shrugged Ali. 'Come on, you can nap in the car on the way there.'

'On the way where?' asked Tulip. 'We didn't get that little detail.'

'Don't have the precise location, I'm still waiting on the intel from SWAT,' said Nan-Nan. 'Get packed, get Witch in the Nan-mobile, and we'll just drive north.'

'Why is Witch coming with us?' asked Ali, watching Witch snake out of the kitchen as she'd spotted an unfortunate bird trilling on the neighbour's wall.

Nan-Nan just grinned. She looked a bit like a cat, too.

CHAPTER 6:
PiT PEOPLE

It turned out that getting Witch into the car was a bit harder than they'd thought.

First of all, they couldn't find her. She'd disappeared on her usual bird hunt after breakfast. Witch was a stray who only came home for food and fun. Nan-Nan had to send the Robo-Cat to look for her, but Witch hissed at it and scratched the camera. She only came back when the mussels were topped off with a can of old tuna and the fish bits from the trash bag, and left in a temptingly stinking pile for her in the back garden.

Then, they couldn't get her into the car. She was happy enough in Tulip's arms, or squashed in Ali's gym bag, but she furiously refused to get into the cat-carrier.

'Why does she need to be in the cat-carrier?' said Tulip, trying to push her in, but Witch just shrieked and scrabbled out with her claws and leapt around the walls in fury, before settling on the kitchen table like a self-satisfied statue.

'It's the law,' complained Nan-Nan, 'and I don't want any police stopping the car. I've got . . . stuff, in there. If they found it, might be hard to harm my way out of it.'

'You mean *charm* your way out of it,' said Tulip.

'I know what I said,' said Nan-Nan.

'She's literally shredded my T-shirt,' complained Ali, inspecting herself in the black mirror of the microwave. 'You can see right down to the T-shirt under it.'

'Looks quite nice,' said Tulip, kindly.

'It does actually, doesn't it?' said Ali, admiring the rips. 'And THAT's why I double dress.'

'Maybe we should just leave her,' said Tulip. 'She thinks she's going to cat prison.'

'Yeah, I wouldn't get into a cage,' said Ali. 'It's

like someone asking you to do the play date in a basement, and then they quietly lock the door at the top of the stairs, and steal your stuff.'

'Which is why my basement has an escape hatch,' said Nan-Nan, 'not that any bad people have ever locked me in there. Ever. Nope. Not at all.'

An hour later, Witch had beaten them. They'd put the stinky fish in the cage as bait, but she just looked at them like they were stupid. And chasing her hissing blur of fur around the house just got them more scratches.

'I've had enough,' said Ali. 'I give up. Stupid fat-cat always has to win.'

'Think she's had enough, too,' said Tulip, nodding towards the hallway. Witch had pawed her way into Ali's gym bag, and was settling down for a nap.

'Stupid mangy moggy, gerroff!' yelled Ali, ready to thunder down the hall, but Tulip grabbed her arm.

'Wait,' she hissed.

Ali shrugged her off. 'It's not your gym kit she's manking up with her fish breath . . .' But she paused, watching Witch curl up into a purring ball and fall fast asleep.

'Oh,' she said. 'Gotcha.'

'Yep,' said Tulip. 'Don't know why you have to make everything so hard, with all your traps and bait and stuff. Didn't need a trap. Just a bit of patience.'

'Sure you don't wanna stitch that on a heart-shaped pillow,' scoffed Ali. But Nan-Nan nodded approvingly, as Tulip gently scooped up Witch in the bag, closed it gently, and popped the bag in the cat-carrier.

'Let's roll,' said Nan-Nan.

'Are we allowed to make wheelchair jokes now?' asked Ali, following her. Tulip thumped her back.

'You gotta work on your sensitivity,' said Tulip.

Ali snorted. She saw Twitch, the Robo-Cat, prowling back towards the house, and pulled a grotesque face at it, like she was pulling off a mask. The Robo-Cat took another shot.

'Oh dear,' laughed Nan-Nan, looking at the picture on her phone. 'You're hideous, munchkin! That one's going on my screen saver.'

On the motorway, Nan-Nan still wasn't giving

them the deets on the destination, even though they'd chanted, 'Are-we-there-yet-are-we-there-yet-are-we-there-yet . . .' since leaving home.

'Enough!' said Nan-Nan. 'You've got to earn the intel. What've you worked out? You've had enough clues.'

'You mean, what's our diagnosis?' asked Tulip.

'Exactly,' said Nan-Nan. 'It's sort of a test.'

'Lucky for us, we rock at tests,' said Ali. 'We don't even need to cheat, we just hide things in our head.'

'That's called studying,' pointed out Tulip.

'You make everything sound noob-ish,' complained Ali.

'So . . . Mum told us the holiday was off,' said Tulip. 'That's how this all started.'

'Hmm, a teensy bit self-centred, that,' said Nan-Nan.

'And we were hanging out on the wall, and Momo had been waiting there with a customer.'

'Better,' said Nan-Nan. 'Any idea why his fare was hanging about on your road?'

'Momo said she was waiting for someone,' said Ali. 'But when she saw us, she was pretty rude. And then she cut Momo on her way out of the cab. Sliced the popliteal artery through his jeans. And we didn't work it out until she was heading round the corner.'

'And?' said Nan-Nan.

'And she had a ginger clown wig, like the one you wear on duty with the SWAT squad,' said Ali.

'And after that it was a bit of a blur, because we were saving Momo's life, and all,' said Tulip, apologetically.

'Plus,' said Ali, not wanting to be outdone, 'you've become a bit kitty-obsessed. You've built some random Robo-Cat to guard the house and take unflattering pics of us. You keep saying "purr-fect". And you insisted on bringing Witch and she's really not your biggest fan at the moment.'

'So you've worked a lot out yourself,' said Nan-Nan, proudly. 'I'd say you've earned the intel, girls. Where do you think we're REALLY staying?' She was turning a corner down a country lane.

There was a sign at the top of the lane. It said, CATTY'S CATTERY. With an enormous picture of a cat, hanging off a pole. With the line, 'Hang on in there.'

'You said it was a hotel,' said Tulip in wonder. 'A horrible purr-fect cat-astrophe of a hotel!'

'It's a cat hotel!' said Ali, spotting another cat poster sign. It was a shot of a grumpy-looking cat, saying, 'No, THIS is my happy face.' 'That's why you needed Witch.'

'I don't think this could get any madder,' said Tulip, looking crossly at Nan-Nan. 'We wanted the holiday. Not Witch. And we can't dump her in a cattery. She's gonna be furious when she wakes up.'

But just then, it did get madder. Nan-Nan got a beeping alert on her phone. She glanced at it and, without warning, did a hard turn left into the woods. They lurched down a dirt track barely wider than the car, towards a clearing in the trees.

And there was a strangely familiar figure lurking there.

A tall woman in a trench coat, with a fedora hat, and with a wig of steel-coloured curls. The SWAT team uniform. The girls had seen this woman once before. She'd crashed Evelyn Sprotland's funeral, which they had to hold without the body, as he'd disappeared into the river.

'Agent Silver,' whispered Tulip. 'Do you remember what she said to us at the funeral?'

Ali nodded, 'That she needed detectives who were medics. That she had a job for us.'

Nan-Nan pulled up sharply next to Silver, close enough to spray her with dirt and gravel from the spinning wheels. Silver didn't flinch or step away, but just frowned and looked at her watch, as though Nan-Nan had taken her time.

'Here and now, Silver?' Nan-Nan said. 'Seriously, I haven't even got the girls their lunch yet.'

'Now and here, Ruby,' said Silver. 'And lunch is for wimps.' She frowned at the girls, too.

'I don't like her,' whispered Tulip. Her tummy was rumbling.

'Don't stress,' said Ali, 'still got a school bag of snacks.' She opened her bag and showed Tulip her back-up packets of Pringles and mini Mars Bars.

'You're brilliant!' said Tulip.

'Nah, just lazy,' admitted Ali. 'I never unpacked it from the last time when we were running away 'cause of Sprotland.'

'Well, yet again, your laziness has paid off,'

said Tulip, grabbing a packet of crisps from the bag and stepping out of the car decisively.

'Don't worry about lunch, Nan-Nan,' said Tulip. 'We're good.'

'Good?' said Silver. 'Yes. Well, your past form would indicate that. But this is a more delicate task than exposing the blundering poison-peddler barging around your school.' She was tapping her foot impatiently. 'Come on, Ruby, get out!'

'Fine,' snapped Nan-Nan, 'but I don't have the all-terrain wheelchair.'

'Yes, yes, you're legless, that's your excuse for everything,' said Silver, yanking out Nan-Nan's chair and setting it up for her. She'd obviously done it before.

'Thanks,' said Nan-Nan. 'Where are the SWAT team?'

'What!' squeaked Tulip. 'You're gonna let us meet the SWAT squad?'

'Finally,' said Ali. 'Took your time.'

'It's your call,' said Nan-Nan. 'But if you tell your mum I'm gonna deny this ever happened.'

'The team are lurking in the woods,' snapped Silver impatiently. 'Apart from Agent Golda, she's getting her second hip replaced, she'll be video-calling in from the hospital.' She began rolling Nan-Nan further down the path.

Tulip and Ali looked at each other. Uncertain whether they should stay or go.

'Spit-spot, girls,' said Nan-Nan, as she rolled past them. 'Make your minds up. We've got a briefing. But once you come, there's no going back. You'll be SWAT sisters, too.'

'I don't like being given ultimatums,' complained Ali. 'I don't like being told what to do.'

'It's the only way to find out who did this to Momo,' Tulip pointed out. 'And it's better with Nan-Nan than not.'

'Fine,' snapped Ali, and they trailed after Nan-Nan and Silver into the woods. 'Do you have biscuits at these things? I'm only up for it if there'll be biscuits,' she called out.

They followed Nan-Nan and Silver into a clearing. There was no one there. It was a bit of an anti-climax.

But then Nan-Nan clapped her hands, and suddenly they were in a circle of trench coats and fedoras. It was like the women of the SWAT team had materialized out of the trees. They clearly liked making an entrance.

'Agent Ebony,' barked a woman, sporting a black wig with extravagant curls bubbling out from under the hat like a Beyoncé weave. 'Reconnaissance undertaken. All clear.'

'Agent Amber,' said another, with a yellow wig. 'Intel received. Ready to brief.' She held out her phone.

'Agent Golda,' crackled another voice, and they could see a woman on Agent Amber's phone screen, it looked like she was in a bathroom. She was hastily cramming on her wig of gold curls under a fedora. 'Hospital subject safe and secure.'

'Hospital subject!' said Tulip. 'That's gotta be Momo.'

Ali nudged Tulip, 'D'you think that the wigs are stitched into the hats?'

'Agent Ivory,' nodded another woman, her curly wig was pure white, and she looked a bit like Mrs Claus. 'Nutrition detail. Biscuits and Tea!' She held out a tray with china cups and custard creams.

'Ooh, you're my favourite agent!' squealed Tulip, running towards her.

'Me first,' said Ali, shouldering her out of

the way. 'In case they're, I dunno, poisoned or something.' She shoved one in her mouth. 'Nope, they're good, you're good.'

'And introducing our new SWAT members,' said Nan-Nan, drily. 'The medical detectives. Their main skill is in their ninja-like stealth and stomachs of steel.'

'Can we have cool names, too?' asked Tulip.

'Sure,' said Nan-Nan. 'How about Detective Cocoa and Detective Brownie?'

'How do we pick which is which?' asked Ali.

'Does it matter?' said Agent Silver, sharply. 'I don't even care which of *you* is which! Let's get on with it, girls.'

'I'll go first,' said Agent Golda. 'There's a woman with an irritable bladder on my ward and I have exactly 200 seconds before she starts banging down this bathroom door.' She pushed her face closer to the screen. 'Subject has regained consciousness. He has confirmed our suspicions. You're looking in the right place. I've got him under surveillance. If a suspicious fire alarm goes off, or someone without clearance enters the subject's ward, I'll know.'

'Great work, Golda,' said Nan-Nan. 'How's the new hip?'

'Swivelling nicely,' said Golda. 'I'll show up the lot of you at the Wednesday training session.'

A banging on the door interrupted her. 'Miss Goldstein, quit bathroom hogging or I'll steal your kosher meal,' squalled a woman outside. 'And who takes a fedora into a bathroom?'

'It's *Professor* Goldstein,' snapped Golda to the woman. 'Golda out!' she said to the camera, and she flicked off the connection.

Agent Amber spoke up, 'Further intel. We checked the sat nav on the victim's cab. It came from the closest village to here.'

'Bit of a coincidence,' said Nan-Nan, 'that the client who attacked him was just a few minutes from the cattery we've had under surveillance for the last few weeks.'

'There are NO coincidences, Ruby,' said Agent Silver with superb authority, staring her down.

'Why are you bothering to put surveillance on a cattery?' asked Ali. 'Because of all the criminal cats? Cat burglars?' She sniggered, while dunking another biscuit. 'Really, no chocolate ones?' she added reproachfully to Agent Ivory.

'They didn't have the Fairtrade bourbons in the local shop,' said Agent Ivory. 'So I went with the vegan custard creams.'

Ali spat out her biscuit. 'This is VEGAN? You're disguising vegetables as biscuits! That's just wrong. That's misrepresentation. That's a CRIME!'

'We've got a real crime to sort,' said Agent Ivory, frowning. 'And that's not how you say thank you. I'm beginning to wonder if we need you.'

Tulip replied crossly, 'So why *do* you need us? Agent Silver said she had a job for us at Sprotland's funeral. A detective-medic job. Not a kitty-sitting job.'

'Good questions,' said Nan-Nan. 'The surveillance is because the cattery's decidedly dodgy. It's been receiving vast injections of cash.'

'Maybe some people died and left their money to the place,' said Ali. 'People are always dying and leaving their cash to cat shelters.'

'Everyone likes cats,' agreed Tulip. 'Unless they like dogs more. That's why cute kitty pictures are all over the internet.'

'This isn't a cat shelter,' snapped Agent Amber. 'It's a cat hotel. But for some reason clients are gifting ALL their money to it, while they're still very much in the world. Lots don't even have pets.'

'Ooh, that's interesting!' said Ali, her eyes shining. 'Blackmail! Extortion! Big stuff!'

'That's where you and Agent Ruby come in,' said Agent Ebony, nodding to the twins and Nan-Nan. 'We need someone undercover to assess what's going on here.'

'And no one's gonna suspect a winsome granny with her beloved moggy, and her two adorable granddaughters,' said Tulip, a bit sarcastically. 'We don't exactly blend in, you can basically see Nan-Nan from space with her big hair and pleather jacket.'

'Negative,' said Agent Ebony. 'I've done a reconnaissance, and no one can see us at all. I've done a sweep for lasers, cameras, drones, tripwires . . .'

Tulip was looking around for a place to put down her teacup so she could start her crisps.

'Hidden bugs, radiation emitting equipment, phone signals . . .'

'Pop it back on the tray, dear,' suggested Agent Ivory.

'WiFi, walkie-talkies, landmines . . .'

'Nah, don't worry, this old log is fine,' said

Tulip. She walked over to it, and promptly disappeared with a whoosh into the ground. Feet first and with a flumpy-thump. There had been a net stretched over a vast hole, at least six feet deep, camouflaged with mulch and leaves. 'Aargh! There's a pit. I'm in a pit!'

'A pit?' said Agent Ebony, looking a bit annoyed. She tossed her bouncing wig of Beyoncé curls. 'Yeah, I just did all the tech reconnaissance. I didn't think to check for holes in the ground. A bit below my pay grade.'

A screeching burglar alarm started sounding out.

'I'm guessing you didn't check for old-fashioned burglar alarms either,' said Nan-Nan, rolling her eyes, and then rolling hurriedly towards Tulip.

'Of course not,' said Agent Ebony, crossly. 'I'm an artist, not a cavewoman.'

Ali ran to Tulip, and promptly disappeared down another mesh-covered hole, which set off another shrieking alarm.

'This place is booby trapped!' she shrieked, tugging herself out of the net that she had got tangled in.

'A hole in the ground with an oversized alarm

clock is hardly a trap,' scoffed Agent Silver, walking briskly towards them. 'More of a child's plaything.' The girls heard a short, sharp cry, and then another flump-thump.

'Sorry, Silver, but did you just fall into the child's plaything?' asked Tulip. She heard Ali snort with laughter.

'Get out of here, team,' said Nan-Nan, commandingly. 'They're coming!'

'Who's they?' yelled Ali and Tulip together. But nobody replied. It seemed everyone else already knew.

Nan-Nan leaned over the edge of Tulip's pit and chucked her a bag. 'Put these clothes on, quick!' she hissed. She did the same for Ali.

Tulip had managed to get her head over the edge of her pit, with a foothold on a stiff bit of root. She saw Agent Silver vault athletically out of the hole where she'd fallen, using a knobbly old branch. She moved pretty sharply for an old lady. The curls of her silver wig were barely displaced under her precisely positioned fedora. And the SWAT team disappeared back up into the trees, and began leaping away through the branches, swinging on grappling hooks they had tugged from their belts. The girls knew that the

SWAT team trained every Wednesday at Nan-Nan's place, but they had never seen them in action.

'Wow,' said Tulip, admiringly. 'The old girls are all as strong as Nan-Nan. And almost as flamboyant.'

'OK,' said Ali grudgingly, 'that's pretty impressive.' She had managed to stick her own head out of the hole and gave Tulip a thumbs-up. 'So I guess this is our life now? We're just gonna have to live here, in the holes. We're basically pit people.' She was actually a bit scared that the agents had just ditched them in the ditch, and swung off to save their own skins, but she wasn't going to admit that.

'At some level,' said Tulip, playing along, 'I always knew it would happen.' She gave a small smile, trying to hide her own panic. 'I'm not scared,' she added, a bit too firmly.

'I'm not either,' said Ali, lifting up her chin defiantly, like it was a competition. 'I'm even MORE not-scared than you.'

'After all, Nan-Nan told the other agents to go,' added Tulip. 'And Nan-Nan knows best, right?'

They looked over to Nan-Nan, who was

hurriedly heading back to the car, wheeling painfully over the uneven ground and cursing the lack of all-terrain wheels.

They heard voices and shots in the distance. Actual shots. They both squeaked with fear, and dropped instinctively back into their pits.

'Briefing's complete, girls!' called Nan-Nan. 'Tell me you're in those costumes! You're SWAT now, no civvies on duty!'

'Well, this is dumb,' complained Ali, scrabbling in the leaves at the bottom of the hole, and finally locating the plastic bag that Nan-Nan had chucked in. She hurriedly tugged on the baggy trousers and the checked shirt in the bag. There was a hat too.

'This is dumber,' said Tulip, already changed, at the bottom of her pit. She inspected the hat, and burst out laughing, despite the shots in the distance and the desperate situation.

There was a curly cocoa-coloured wig sewn into it.

CHAPTER 7:
CATTY'S CATTERY

There was another shot. Tulip stopped laughing abruptly, and rammed the hat on her head. And then there was a screech, and they heard Witch hissing and shrieking as she leapt wildly from the car. They could see her bouncing off the trees with fury, almost as athletically as the SWAT ladies.

'Nan-Nan let her out?' said Tulip. 'Why?'

Then they heard Nan-Nan's voice. Except she sounded like a sweet little old lady. 'Oh-my-gosh, thank goodness you've come, you've got to save my little ones!'

'Worra-you-doin-creeping-bout-the-cattery?' growled an unfriendly voice.

'We were just looking for our cat,' yelled Tulip, suddenly realizing why Nan-Nan had let Witch out.

'Then we fell in your stupid big hole, you know, the one that's not in your stupid big face!' yelled Ali. 'Get us out.'

'Oh, I'm sure these kind, strong, gorilla-sized gentlemen aren't responsible for the holes,' said Nan-Nan sweetly. 'They could be anyone's holes.'

'Um, yeah,' said another gruff voice, sounding shifty, 'anyone's.'

Ali looked up, and saw a big greasy face staring down at her.

'Hang on, mate,' he said to her gruffly. 'I'll get the ladder orf the van.'

'Not your mate,' snapped Ali.

Ali and Tulip climbed up and out of the holes. They looked each other up and down like they were looking in a mirror.

They were both in baggy jeans with rips, and chains, and baggy checked shirts. They were both in baseball caps with short, curly wigs.

They looked like . . .

'BOY-oh-boy,' said Nan-Nan in that weird quavery voice. 'I was so worried about you, my darling little men.' Her wheelchair had been put away, and she was leaning on a stick. She was looking like she'd nicked Silver's mop of steel-grey curls. She was wearing big glasses with silver frames, with a chain to hang them around her neck. And she'd put on a massive frothy-flowery dress that hid her skinny jeans. Her leather jacket had been replaced with a pastel cardigan. She looked NOTHING like Nan-Nan. The only giveaways were her shiny boots, that peeped out from under her frilly hem, and the red lipstick, which she was hastily wiping away.

'Hey, Granny,' said Tulip sweetly. 'Seen any big bad wolves in the woods, recently?'

Ali guffawed. 'She looks SO much like the gran-gran in Red Riding Hood.'

'No big bad wolves. Only big strong heroes,' said Nan-Nan, looking with revolting gratitude at the greasy-faced guy who'd got them out, and his shifty Frankenstein-sized sidekick.

'Yeah, well the cattery needs security, innit,' said Greasy-Faced Guy. 'We heard there was something going on in the woods.'

'Our cat's not used to car journeys,' said Tulip. 'We let her out so she wouldn't puke inside, but she escaped.'

'Here, kitty,' said Ali, unconvincingly, to the trees. 'Nope?' She turned to the goons. 'Well, I tried. She's your cat, now. Congratulations.'

'You lads stay here and get her down,' said Greasy-Faced Guy. 'We'll give your granny a ride to reception. Can you drive that thing down the path?' he added, nodding towards the Nan-mobile.

'Ooh, probably,' said Ali excitedly. 'Can we?'

'They're ten,' snapped Nan-Nan, before she remembered herself and went back into wavery-voiced character. 'Best not, dears, your Legoland driving passes expired last year.'

'Then you'd better follow us in the car,' Greasy said to Nan-Nan. 'You lads,' he said, pointing to the girls, 'get that cat and walk down to Catty's Cattery. Path's that way.'

'Gotcha,' said Tulip.

'Wotcha,' said Ali, spitting at the ground.

Tulip thought that was a nice touch.

When the goons and Nan-Nan had driven off,

Tulip and Ali were left staring at each other in their new outfits.

'You think it's weird that Nan-Nan's disguised us as boys?' said Tulip. 'It's not like SHE had to be a boy.'

'Doesn't even come into my top ten of weird,' shrugged Ali. 'Maybe Nan-Nan couldn't find SWAT trench coats in our size. What's weird is how easily they believed it.'

'Why wouldn't they?' said Tulip.

Witch had been hovering indecisively overhead on a tree branch, as though she was unsure who they were too.

'Here, Witchy!' called Tulip.

'Suppose you're right,' said Ali. 'Why would anyone pretend to be a BOY if they weren't? Yeuch.'

Tulip shook her head sadly, 'You're just a big ball of prejudice,' she said. 'Like we're so awesome?'

Ali looked Tulip up and down, with a smirk. 'Well, I am.' She spat at the ground again.

'You can stop doing that gross spitting-bit, now,' said Tulip. 'It was pretty convincing as an act.'

'What act?' said Ali, with genuine surprise.

She hawked up another bit of gunk.

'Wow, you're just gross,' muttered Tulip, stalking off towards Witch's tree.

'Aww, thank you,' said Ali. She adjusted her hair-hat, and watched Tulip beckon again towards Witch with a here-Witchy-Witchy-Witchy. The cat leapt easily into Tulip's arms. Ali felt an odd tug of jealousy. Of course Witch liked Tulip more than her. Everyone liked Tulip more than her. Stupid-kind-caring Tulip.

'There, there, Witchy,' said Tulip, nuzzling her. 'Nothing to be afraid of.'

'She's on her way to a cat prison,' said Ali, 'guarded by greasy guys with guns. Nothing to be afraid of at all.'

The girls waited around for a bit, in case any of the agents came back. But it seemed that they were long gone. They started following the path back to the road, found another dangling cat poster, this time with the headline 'Cat-astrophe!', and carried on. The weird thing, as they approached Catty's Cattery, was that it didn't seem like their idea of a cattery at all. It seemed more like a derelict holiday camp. There were elderly people tottering around the shabby grounds, or sitting on benches with their oxygen tanks plugged into their nostrils, playing cards. There was a bowls area on fake astro turf, with ancient gentlemen in white, rolling balls along the ground in what seemed like slow motion, but was probably normal motion for them. There was a skeletally thin woman leading a yoga class on a mat by a green-tinged pool, with cracked tiles and moss leaking out of the edges. At least the cats weren't locked away, there were a fair few moggies sprawled around like they were on holiday, too. Looking as elderly as their owners. An almost hairless one was peering curiously into the pool, like he was hopeful for fish.

'Hey, this place has a pool!' said Tulip, excitedly.

'It's got pseudomonas, too,' said Ali, inspecting the water critically, the bubbling green bacteria stank like old washing-up water. 'A dip in there might just finish off these old cat-lovers.'

CHECK PAGE 301 OF THE APPENDIX FOR THE MINI-MEDIX BLOG POST
TWINTERMISSION! BACTERIA HYSTERIA
OR THE PSEUDOMONAS EXPERIMENT

'Where are the cat cages?' asked Tulip, holding Witch protectively.

'Dunno,' shrugged Ali. 'Maybe the whole place is like an open enclosure, like at the zoo.'

Witch slithered out of Tulip's arms, unimpressed. She stalked past the other cats, like they weren't cool enough for her to hang out with, and started grooming herself disdainfully.

'Poor Witchy,' said Tulip. 'It's like first day at a new school for her. I hope she makes some friends.'

Ali looked at Tulip, open-mouthed with disbelief. 'THAT's your big concern at the moment. Seriously?'

'Well, we've never had to fly solo,' said Tulip. 'Feel sorry for kids who do.'

'Twins!' called Nan-Nan, over by the largest of the derelict buildings dotted around the grounds. The Greasy Face and Frankenstein goons who'd found them in the woods were standing on each side of her like bodyguards. The Nan-mobile was parked roughly on the muddy track that led from the main road. 'Spit-spot.'

Tulip's phone started ringing. 'It's Zac,' she said.

Ali's phone started ringing. 'It's Jay,' she said, swiping to DENIED.

'Hey, it might be important,' said Tulip. She went to answer her phone, but Ali took it from her and swiped off the call.

'You'll blow the cover,' said Ali. 'Not the time to start chattering away to Dum-Dum and Dumber. Call them when we're alone.'

Tulip was annoyed that Ali was probably right. She quickly messaged: SOZ, LATERS. WE'RE BOYZ UNDERCOVER + CAN'T TALK. UNLESS IT'S LIFE AND DEATH.

Zac messaged back straight away. IT'S LIFE AND DEATH.

'What!' said Tulip, staring at the screen.

Ali grabbed her phone and looked at the message disdainfully.

'Gah, that kid's so needy. Nobody likes needy,' she said, and stomped towards Nan-Nan.

''Sup?' she said, with one of those arrogant head jerks, like a reverse nod. Copying the shirtless older boys on bikes at school, the ones who hung out at the bus stops, and who terrorized the shopkeepers.

Again, Tulip had to admire the commitment

to the boy bit.

''Sup?' she echoed, sticking out her chin and standing in a power stance.

'You constipated, dears?' said Nan-Nan. 'Come on, apparently we're checking in. That's what these charming gentlemen are expecting us to do.'

'What is this place, really?' whispered Tulip, as the goons moved back to their banged-up four wheel drive. Probably to re-set their traps in the woods to stop stray strangers coming to the clearing. 'And who's checking in? Us or the cat?'

'That,' said Nan-Nan, 'is what we're about to find out. It's clearly no ordinary cattery, just as we thought. I'm doubting it's a cattery at all.'

'It's more like a pet-friendly budget holiday camp,' agreed Tulip. 'A cat-themed hostel. Deffo smells like wet cat.'

'Great, we're trapped in the woods in the kitty-obsessed-hotel-from-hell,' said Ali, looking around dismissively. 'Purr-fect.'

'More like cat-astrophe,' said Tulip, remembering the poster. 'What? That was a joke,' she said, as both Ali and Nan-Nan stared at her.

'Oh no, dear,' said Nan-Nan. 'That wasn't a joke.'

'Jokes are funny,' explained Ali.

Tulip gathered up Witch, and they went into the narrow entrance, choked with ivy, with Nan-Nan struggling convincingly with her cane and her screw-on legs. Behind the reception desk stood a man with his back to them, shuffling bits of paper. There was an old-fashioned service bell on the desk, next to a massive book of tattered leather, with 'Reservations' written on the cover in faded gold.

'Hey,' said Ali, slamming her hand on the bell. She couldn't resist pressing buttons.

'Yes?' said the man helpfully, turning around.

Tulip and Ali couldn't believe it. Nan-Nan gave a sharp intake of breath.

'SPROTLAND!' they said together.

CHAPTER 8:
SPROTLAND'S DOUBLE

The man leaned over, placed his fingers lightly on the reservations book, and flicked through it efficiently.

'Really?' he said, with mild confusion. 'You seem very certain. But I don't think I've got your reservation. Nothing for Sprotland. Is that you or the cat? There always seems to be a bit of confusion about that, when guests first arrive.'

'Go for STURGEON!' said Ali sarcastically. Brian Sturgeon was the identity that Sprotland had stolen for his recent crime spree.

The man looked a bit bewildered, but then his

eyes settled on the novelty singing fish stuck on the wall next to him. It was below another cat poster, with the legend, 'Live while you have life to live, give while you have cash to give'.

He smiled, 'Oh, no, boys, that's a singing salmon, I think. Not a sturgeon. Awful, isn't it?'

'Boys?' said Ali, raising an eyebrow. 'It's US, Sturgeon.' She'd spent weeks ignoring him while he'd been their mum's boyfriend, living in their old playroom. It was pretty annoying having to try to get his attention now.

'Oh, sorry, you're the Sturgeons, are you?' said the man, frowning as he ran a finger down the hand-written ledger. 'Don't think we've got that name down, either. Did you phone in your booking? Maybe the boss forgot to tell me. Sorry.'

'Oh no, dear,' said Nan-Nan, limping forward convincingly. '*We're* sorry. My people must've forgotten to book.' She put a trimmed nail on the ledger. 'Write us in now, if you'd be so kind. Lady Rubina and family.'

'But . . .' said Tulip, crossing her arms, gaping at the man like he was a ghost. 'But, that's . . .'

Nan-Nan shook her head, imperceptibly. It was crazy. Evil Evelyn Sprotland was standing right there, and Nan-Nan was acting like it was no big deal. Normal Nan-Nan behaviour would be to knock him out and sit on him.

'We're a bit late,' said Nan-Nan. 'Got lost in the woods. Chasing our cat. Your delightful groundskeepers helped us out.'

'Think you mean EVIL henchmen,' sniffed Tulip.

'Oh, very good,' laughed the man. 'Evil henchmen, ha! I wish they were efficient enough to be henchmen. I've had them digging holes in the woods just to keep them busy. They're not expensive but they do annoy the residents.'

Ali and Tulip looked at each other.

One of those unspoken conversations, with a furious glare, and wide questioning eyes, and a *That's Mad*, and *I-Know-Right*.

The guy behind the desk was definitely Sprotland.

But he also wasn't.

Same height. Same face. Same brown eyes.

Maybe the same voice, even. It was hard to tell, as this man was being polite, but Sprotland was always sneering or telling them to go to bed.

Just the hair was different—a bit longer than before. Otherwise, all that was missing was the stupid hat and shades combo that Sprotland had worn, to conceal his real identity.

They knew him. But the weird thing was, he obviously didn't know them. Didn't know Nan-Nan, either. Their disguises weren't *that* good.

'All in order,' said the man. 'I'll show you to your room.'

'So definitely not a cat cage?' asked Tulip, whispering the last word so Witch wouldn't hear. Witch had bounced on the desk, and was pawing the plastic Singing Salmon with obvious disappointment.

'A bit uncalled for,' said the man. 'We make the rooms rather nice, given the circumstances.' He gathered a pair of clanking keys, and nodded efficiently. 'Follow me, and do bring your kitty.'

Ali couldn't understand it. And then with a burst of inspiration, she said, 'You're not *the* Sprotland. You're *a* Sprotland! There are more of you. Didn't think your type managed to reproduce.'

The man stiffened. 'Now, that,' he said, 'is truly uncalled for, young sir. I'm beginning to think that *Sprotland* is street slang for something less than polite.'

'Sorry,' said Nan-Nan. She skewered Ali with

a look of pure steel. 'It's an innocent schoolyard phrase. A Sprotland just means, rather clever.'

The man looked uncertain about this.

'Well, I suppose I'm not down with the kids,' he admitted, striding on through the decrepit building.

'You know what gave that away?' sniggered Ali. 'Saying down with the kids.'

'Behave, boys,' said Nan-Nan, mildly. She seemed to think that they'd got away with it. Whatever it was. Tulip was still pretty unsure about who was playing who, but decided to go along with it.

They came to the end of a long, windowless corridor.

'You've lucked out,' said the man-who-looked-like-Sprotland. 'You get the corner suite. Views on both sides of the building.'

'Is the view different?' asked Tulip.

'Oh certainly,' said the man enthusiastically. 'On the north side, there are conifers and on the east side there are horse chestnuts and a feisty yew.'

'So basically, trees or trees,' said Ali, pushing past the man once he'd clanked open the worn-out door. He barely needed to unlock it, she could have kicked it in without too much effort.

'Oh,' said Tulip, looking around. 'That's disappointing.'

Nan-Nan and Ali looked pretty disappointed too. She wasn't quite sure what they'd thought they'd find in the mysterious hidden hotel, but a grotty room with peeling wallpaper and a damp patch on the ceiling, with a steel bed and a metal bunkbed with threadbare towels dumped on them, wasn't exactly top of their list. There was a single lightbulb dangling from the ceiling, and a depressed-looking spider descending listlessly. Witch jumped out of Tulip's arms in disgust and stalked away.

'You see,' said the man, striding towards the window, and pushing away a printed curtain on rattling rings, 'lovely views!' He sounded sincere.

Nan-Nan had been oddly quiet, taking in the room. Looking at the man. 'You died,' she said, pointedly.

'What?' said the man, utterly confused.

And then Nan-Nan did something strange. She grinned. 'Silly sausage, sir,' she said. 'I mean the YEW died.' She nodded towards the window.

'Oh,' he said. 'Well, it's rather wet here. Probably got soggy roots. I've noticed that the Weeping Willow is doing VERY well.'

Tulip looked out the window, and saw a woman stomping across the grounds, dressed in long flowing clothes, with an oversized sunhat and sunglasses, like she was avoiding the paparazzi. The man raised his hand to the woman, but she ignored him.

'That's Catty, she's very busy,' he said, a bit too hastily.

Tulip nodded. No one liked being publicly blanked. Even in front of two kids and a stranger.

He left the key on the bed. There wasn't any other furniture. 'Bathroom is down the hall. Mealtimes are pinned on your door. Fire exit is through the window.'

He turned and bowed at the door. 'Welcome to Catty's Cattery. The residence to stay and play for all your days.'

CHAPTER 9:
MODUS OPERANDI

'Wow,' said Ali, throwing herself on the single bed. 'Most stupid name for a hotel, ever. Catty's Cattery.'

'Bit egotistical,' agreed Tulip, 'naming a place after yourself.'

'There's a lot to unpack here,' said Nan-Nan, still at the window, pulling the curtain shut decisively.

'And we're not even talking about the baggage,' added Tulip. 'Was that him? I'm not sure. He's literally Sprotland's spitting image, but . . .'

'But Sprotland's not that good an actor,' finished Ali. 'He deffo didn't know us. I mean, I can get him not recognizing ONE of us, but put us together, and we're a bit of a package. Two kids and a lame old lady.'

'Hey,' snapped Nan-Nan, 'enough with the lame old. I'd rather get old than the alternative. And we're in pretty good disguises. You changed gender and I went from wheels of steel to lead legs.' She shoved Ali off the bed, and sat there herself, unscrewing her legs. 'Gah, these are sore,' she complained, massaging the stumps.

'Whadya gonna say those prongs are, if the guy comes snooping?' asked Ali, climbing up the bunkbed. 'Called it!' She grinned down towards Tulip. 'Top bunk.'

'Hey!' said Tulip, who'd been helping Nan-Nan put away her metal legs. 'No fair.'

'I'll say they're kitchen utensils,' shrugged Nan-Nan, 'for making mincemeat out of my enemies.'

'This place is so full of creep that it probably wouldn't even register on their creepy scale,' said Ali. 'That guy who's JUST LIKE Sprotland — what's your diagnosis?' She looked at Tulip.

'Bang on the head?' suggested Tulip. 'He took

a bit of a dive into the river. Maybe he washed up not knowing who he was? And ended up taking a job running . . . whatever this is?'

'Nah, more likely he's another Sprotland, like I said,' insisted Ali. 'Some long lost cousin of Evelyn's.'

'He'd never heard the word before,' said Tulip. 'He can't be a Sprotland.'

'Diagnosis Doppelganger?' suggested Nan-Nan. 'Well, they say everyone has a double, somewhere.'

'Nah,' grinned Tulip. 'Well, not you at least. You're an original.'

'Like we're evidently not,' grumped Ali. She was staring at the ceiling. Mould was blooming from it. 'Ugh, Nan-Nan,' she said. 'Diagnosis Disgusting. I'm sleeping in the car tonight.'

'Catch up,' said Nan-Nan, 'we're not here to stay and play. The job's to find out why people are leaving all their money to this place. And if it's linked to Momo's attacker.'

Nan-Nan's phone started buzzing. She glanced at it. 'Just your mum,' she said, rejecting the call. Then she obviously felt guilty, as she messaged a heart emoji. 'All good, just checking in with the girls,' she said out loud, while she tapped rapidly on the screen.

'So, this is the plan,' she began, but then Ali's phone started buzzing.

'Still Mum,' she said. 'Lady must be keen.' She rejected the call too, with a flamboyant wave emoji, and the 'Smell Ya Later' gif she kept on standby.

And then Tulip's phone starting ringing.

'Haha,' said Ali. 'She rang you after me, she's heading down the ranks.'

'It's not Mum, it's Zac again,' said Tulip. She felt a pang of guilt that she hadn't called him back sooner. The Sprotland stooge had thrown her. 'He said it was a matter of life and death.'

'Knowing Zac, life and death means there's a spider stuck in the bath that he's trying to rescue,' scoffed Ali, but even she looked a bit unsure.

'Hey, Zac,' said Tulip, answering the call. 'Sorry about before. We were just . . .' She stopped to listen. Her mouth fell open, and she covered it with her hand.

Ali wanted to make a joke about fly-catching but something about Tulip's expression stopped her. Instead she went over, and put her arm around her.

'OK,' said Tulip. 'Where are you? We'll come and get you.' She put down her phone, and when she looked up, her eyes were like puddles.

'It's their dad. He's been stabbed in the leg. Just like Momo.'

'Was he helping an old lady?' asked Nan-Nan.

'Yes. How'd you know?' said Tulip.

'Yeah, how DID you know?' said Ali suspiciously.

'Two letters,' said Nan-Nan. 'M and O. And I'm not spelling Momo.'

'Motive and opportunity?' suggested Ali.

'Modus Operandi,' said Nan-Nan. 'I'm thinking there's a pattern.'

'While you two are being all clever,' said Tulip furiously, 'the boys are scared and alone in A&E! Mum's stuck operating in theatre, while you're smelling her later, and BOTH of Zac and Jay's parents are in hospital. If we don't look after the boys, they're gonna call in social services and put them in some sort of emergency care.'

'I'll go and get them,' said Nan-Nan, briskly. She began rapidly messaging on her phone. 'You two, stay here. You can find out a bit more about this place. But just online. Hotel reviews, client comments, that sort of thing. Don't leave this room. Don't talk to that Sprotland lookalike, don't talk to ANYONE.'

'Got it,' said Ali. 'Don't leave the room. Don't talk to anyone.'

'You're leaving us?' said Tulip.

'We can't ALL flounce out the moment we've walked in,' said Nan-Nan. 'They'd smell a fish.'

'Nah, that's just me,' admitted Ali. 'Kept some trash-snacks in my pockets for Witch.'

'Well, it's just a bit irresponsible,' huffed Tulip. 'Abandoning us with the double of a criminal in a creepy place.'

'Oh, sweetie,' said Nan-Nan, giving her a hug. 'Of course it is. Honestly, sometimes it's like you've just met me.'

The moment Nan-Nan left, Tulip pulled her phone out. 'The poor boys,' she said, rapidly texting them. 'You know, this place has a great signal. For the middle of nowhere.' Message sent, she lay back on the lower bunk and began looking through the review websites. Catty's Cattery was a bit of a ghost place online. The only presence was a really basic website for bookings, with cat pictures and no address. No reviews. No nothing. It really wasn't clear that it was for people, and not for cats. Like they were deliberately being confusing.

The whole thing was odd, Tulip thought. Usually there was some stuff online, even if a place was really rubbish.

'D'you think someone's been deleting any mention of this place?' she asked.

'Right, Nan-Nan's gone,' said Ali, hanging down from the bed like the cat in the poster. 'You can stop dweebing about on that. You look like the sad computer guy in the action movie. You know, the one who eats pizza in his shorts and looks up security codes.'

She jumped down and, fixing her curly wig under her cap, she turned the clanky key, and opened the door.

'Whadya doing?' said Tulip.

'What Nan-Nan said,' grinned Ali. 'Leave the room. Talk to anyone.'

'That's not what she said,' sighed Tulip, getting up.

'Pretty sure it was,' said Ali. 'Definitely. She definitely said exactly those words. I've got proof.' With a smirk, Ali played the recorded conversation back from her phone. She'd deleted the *don't* from Nan-Nan's lecture.

'Leave the room. Talk to anyone.'

Ali tutted thoughtfully, 'Anyone? Poor old Nan-Nan could be a bit more precise in her instructions. Forget she's getting on a bit. I'll start with the Sprotland.'

'Nope,' said Tulip. She was still smarting about being called the computer guy. 'I'LL start with him. People like me a load more than they do you.'

'Hah,' said Ali, annoyed because it was true. 'Fine, you keep him busy. Get the backstory. And I'll nose about behind the desk.'

CHAPTER 10:
MEETING MUMSY

Tulip fixed her own unruly wig under the cap, and looked at herself in the black mirror of her phone. She wasn't sure she was as convincingly boy-like as Ali, so she tried a scowl. Nope, she just looked constipated. Then she tried a frown. Better. She tugged up her jeans, and followed Ali out of the room.

The man was clanking a bucket and pail down the dank corridor. He was mopping the floors. Not in a frenzied clean-the-crime-scene way, but in a distracted, domestic way. He was humming to himself.

Tulip couldn't remember ever seeing Evelyn Sprotland do anything helpful around the house. She walked past him, and jerked her chin up, "Sup?' she said.

'Er, 'sup?' repeated the man, like it was a new foreign word he was trying out.

Ali gave a thumbs-up to Tulip behind the man's back, and slid down the corridor silently in her socks, back towards reception. 'Keep him busy,' she mouthed.

'Sorry about the misunderstanding, back there,' said Tulip.

'Oh, no trouble at all, young man,' said the man, continuing to mop. 'What misunderstanding?' he asked, a moment later.

Tulip stared at him, hard. Closer up, he looked even more like Sprotland. If he'd had a hat and shades on, she wouldn't even be second guessing herself. She'd be calling the police. 'Come on,' she said. 'You know.'

'What?' said the man.

'It's me,' Tulip said insistently. 'And you're . . . YOU.'

'Can you smell fish?' asked the man, sniffing around in the direction Ali's whiffy pockets had wafted.

'Just a Sturgeon,' said Tulip.

'You and your brother seem a little obsessed with those,' commented the man. He carried on mopping.

Tulip stared at him, again. He had one of those stupid little beards, but she supposed that Sturgeon could have grown it since his fall in the river. As a sort of disguise. But his hair was too long to have grown since they last saw him. Perhaps it was a wig, like hers. His voice was pretty similar to Sturgeon's too, but the words he was using were completely different. The tone, too. He was being nice. That word hadn't even been in Stupid Sturgeon-Sprotland's vocabulary. She couldn't shake the doubt.

She knew it had been a few weeks, and that you could forget people. But the people who lived in your house, and tried to poison your mum and your school. Well, those were the people you really ought to remember.

'Do you have a tattoo?' she asked him suddenly. Sprotland had tattooed his collarbone in a wildly misjudged attempt to pass himself off as the brain surgeon whose identity he'd stolen.

'Loads,' said the man. 'I've even got one that says *tattoo*. Thought it was clever at the time.'

'Can I see?' asked Tulip, looking interested.

'Sure,' said the man mildly, pushing up his sleeve and revealing a tattoo of *tattoo* in gothic script, surrounded by thorns. 'The others are on my legs.'

Tulip sighed. Either he was diabolically calm, or he really wasn't the bad guy. He just didn't know her. He didn't have a single tell about the things that Sprotland should have been anxious about.

And how could *he* have forgotten her? She'd foiled his plans and got him dumped in the river. THAT was the sort of person you really ought to remember.

Diagnosis Double? Diagnosis Distant Relative? Diagnosis Dive-Induced-Amnesia? It was the uncertainty that was worrying her. It was the not knowing that felt dangerous.

'Maybe you can help me with something, Mr . . .' Tulip paused. She realized she didn't know what to call him. His badge just said Manager in a bright, bouncy font, with a smiley face over the Catty's Cattery logo. 'Sir,' she finished.

'Oh come now,' laughed the man, 'only my mother calls me sir.' He held out his hand. 'It's Manfred. But just call me Manny. Manny Gers.'

'You're called Manny Gers?' asked Tulip, in disbelief.

'It's a French surname, actually,' said the man. 'That's why the G is soft, like the J in jerk. And the S is silent. So you pronounce it . . .'

'Like Manny-ger,' said Tulip. 'And then you became a manager.'

'Never thought of that,' said Manny.

'It's called Nominative Determinism,' said Tulip. 'You become like your name.'

'So what's your name?' asked Manny.

'Oh, um,' said Tulip. She didn't know what her boy-name was meant to be. She supposed it would have been in the SWAT briefing if she hadn't fallen down the hole. 'I'd rather not say.'

'Embarrassing, is it?' said Manny, sympathetically. 'Can't be as bad as Manfred.'

'My friends call me Zac,' said Tulip. 'Just a nickname.' She cursed herself for not coming up with something cooler. Like DragonFire or LaserShark.

'You been here long, Manny?' she asked.

'Not at all,' he said. 'This is a new gig for me. Just started a few weeks back. Needed a fresh start.' He patted his pockets, and located a chocolate bar. 'Here you go, Zac, go share this with your brother. What's his name?'

'Oh, you can call him Jay,' said Tulip. 'Warning you, though, he won't like it.'

Tulip found Ali poring over her phone in the garden. 'Thought you were doing some detective work while I distracted the manager?' she said.

'Duh, I did that ages ago,' said Ali. 'You were chatting forever. So now you're besties with the baddie?'

'He's weirdly pleasant,' said Tulip. 'And I still don't know if he's *him* or not. If he is, he's got no memory and he's had a personality transplant.'

'Reckon the top differential is a hard knock on the head,' said Ali, playing fighty-sock-puppets with her hands. 'Would explain why he never SURFACED afterwards?' she grinned. 'C'mon, surfaced, that was good.'

'But if he's got amnesia, why's he here? Exactly where the SWAT team are investigating. Agent Silver's right, too much of a coincidence.'

'Money?' suggested Ali. 'Maybe someone made him an offer he couldn't refuse.' She showed her phone screen to Tulip. She'd found the public record of Catty's Cattery as a business, with estimated income from charitable donations.

'Following the money,' nodded Tulip. 'Wow. This place is raking it in, considering how rank it is. And the name is completely misleading.' She nodded to the Catty's Cattery sign above the entrance.

'Yeah,' said Ali. 'They should just call it *Cattery*.' She said it with a ta-da flourish of her hands. 'Neater.'

'*That's* what's wrong with it?' sighed Tulip. 'It's a cheap hotel for people that's posing online as a posh hotel for cats. It's getting way too much cash from the guests. And there aren't enough cats about. If it's just a front, they're not really committing to the kitty bit.'

'Can't blame them,' said Ali promptly. 'Cats are a bit full of themselves. Look at Witchy.'

'And look at you, Ali-Cat,' laughed Tulip. 'C'mon, let's go talk to some people, while Manny Gers is busy.'

'What's he calling himself, anyway?' asked Ali.

'Just told you,' said Tulip. 'Manny Gers.'

Ali laughed out loud. 'That's just classic,' she said. 'Even with a knock on the head Sprotland's got zero subtlety. A Brain Surgeon called Brian

Sturgeon and now a Manager called Manny Gers.'

'Oh,' said Tulip, as an old gentleman approached across the bowls lawn, wearing flamboyant white flares and a sequinned waistcoat, 'almost forgot, I named us. I'm Zac and you're Jay.'

'What!' exploded Ali.

'What's up, *Jay*?' said Tulip. 'Be cool.'

'Hello, young men,' said the old gentleman. His hands were shaking as he navigated his way around some gnarled rose bushes, so he pushed them firmly into his pockets. 'Who are you visiting?'

'We're with our Nan-Nan,' said Tulip. 'She's had to pop out.'

'Suppose you want to tell us about the war?' asked Ali, bluntly.

'Oh, I would do, but I've forgotten which one I was in,' said the old gentleman. 'I'm LeRoi. Nice to see some new faces here. Was rather hoping you'd be up for playing some board games.'

'Can we play for money?' asked Ali. 'That's the motto of this place. Saw it on the cat poster. Give while you have cash to give.'

'Oh absolutely,' said the gentleman, 'can't

take it with me. Let's make it interesting.' He gestured towards a chipped picnic table in the weedy grass, with a stack of games piled onto it. His eyes twinkled as much as his waistcoat.

An hour later, there was a cheering crowd of old dears around Ali and Tulip, while Ali brushed the sweat from her forehead and, biting her lip, picked up the tweezers from the Operation board. She confidently approached the brain.

'Jay, Jay, Jay!' shouted the crowd.

'His hands are shaking,' scoffed LeRoi. 'And I know shaking, I've got essential tremor.'

'Nice try, old man,' said Ali. 'YOU picked Operation, not me. Guessing you've been through a few. 'Cause you're so crumbly.'

'Quit trash-talking the nice old residents,' said Tulip nervously. The severe-looking Catty woman whom they had spotted out of the window was approaching them. She was now wearing a trench coat that looked a bit familiar.

'You haven't got the nerve for this game,' goaded LeRoi.

'Least my nerves work,' said Ali, suddenly waggling her hands. 'Shaking or faking?'

'Ooh, please stop mocking the neurological

symptoms of the elderly,' groaned Tulip.

'Nonsense. About time LeRoi's rule of terror was ended,' said a skinny old lady. 'His hands don't shake AT ALL. I've had enough of him grifting us.'

'Well who knew that a sprat would be so good at Operation?' complained LeRoi.

'My mama does this stuff in her sleep,' said Ali.

'WHAT did you say?' said Catty. She was standing behind Ali, frowning down disapprovingly at the shredded jeans and the top of her baseball cap. Tulip looked at Catty sharply. She still had on her enormous movie star shades, with a scarf over her hair. There was nothing unusual about that. Lots of the women had scarves over their hair. Some were quite obviously bald underneath, or wearing wigs. But there was something forced and fake about her accent that Tulip didn't like. It was too high and plummy. She didn't even like the way she was standing, looming over the table.

Witch didn't like her either. She had approached the table, with a group of skinny cats that had decided to follow her about, clearly impressed by the dead bird in her mouth. Witch spat out some feathers while she stared at the woman.

'What does your mother do, son?' pressed Catty.

Ali looked at Tulip, who shook her head, very slightly. They both knew that Ali shouldn't answer the question truthfully, but they weren't sure why.

'Jay, Jay, Jay!' shouted the geriatric crowd. 'Go on, my lad, finish him!'

'She's just very handy,' said Ali, confidently stabbing the tweezers into the head and pulling out the grey brain. She brandished it triumphantly.

There was cheering from the crowds.

'Gah!!!' said LeRoi, pushing himself up from the table. His fake hand tremors had gone.

'You play, you pay,' crowed Ali.

'I would've gotten away with it too,' muttered LeRoi, 'if it wasn't for you pesky kids.' He pulled out coins from his pockets.

'Kids?' said Catty, who hadn't spotted Tulip. 'Kids, plural?' She turned around, and Tulip instinctively ducked under the table. She really didn't want to have a conversation with that woman, she was literally throwing shade on Ali as she lurked behind her, like a villain in an alley.

Witch spat out the bird on the woman's nice, but rather large, shoes.

'Yeeuch!' Catty shrieked. 'Disgusting felines!' She stomped away towards the bench by the bowls court to scrape the feathery goop off her shoes.

'You pesky kids!' said Tulip, petting Witch under the table. 'Ooh, I've always wanted someone to say that to us!'

'You're lucky we only bet the stuff that jingles,' said Ali graciously to LeRoi, 'I usually go for the stuff that folds.'

LeRoi grinned. 'You deserve it,' he said, handing over a fistful of coins.

'Yes,' called out Catty, rubbing at her bird-stained shoes, 'I think he deserves whatever he gets, too.' She gave Ali a dark look through her oversized shades, squinting at her in the sunlight

'Who are you, anyway?' said Ali crossly, standing up.

'Who are you?' asked Catty.

'Not sure that's any of your business,' said Ali.

'I think you'll find that this place is *exactly* my business,' hissed Catty. 'You seem a bit muddled.'

'Not as muddled as your make-up,' snapped Ali. 'Didya get a cement fixer to spray that stuff on you?'

Catty opened her lipsticked mouth in outrage, but at that moment Manny came bustling out, carrying a tray of tea to the bowls players.

'Oh, Mumsy, I see you've met our newest guest family,' he said.

'Mumsy?' frowned Catty.

'Sorry, I meant, boss, Mumsy,' said Manny.

'Yes. The BOSS. So you see, young man,' said Catty smugly to Ali, 'it really is my business, who comes here. AND the manner of their leaving . . .'

She took a cup of tea and swanned off, trench coat swishing behind her. Tulip crawled out from under the table, as Witch hissed at Catty's back, like there weren't enough dead birds in the world to spit at her.

'So, she's nice,' said Ali. 'If it was Opposite Day, and nice meant nasty.'

'That's your *mum*?' Tulip said flatly to Manny. She was trying hard not to do the pity face.

Manny laughed nervously. 'Mumsy just likes her little jokes,' he said. 'She's honestly very caring about our residents. Spends time with all of them. Does their paperwork, even. You know, all their bills . . .'

'And all their wills?' asked Tulip, frowning.

'How did you know?' he asked. 'I think it's nice of her. Given that so many who come to Catty's Cattery don't actually leave here.' Manny had a bit of a gift for saying creepy things like they were perfectly normal.

'I've got a few follow-up questions to that,' started Ali. 'Why don't people leave? And why don't . . .' But then Tulip's phone buzzed.

'Sorry, gotta go,' Tulip said urgently. 'Message from our granny. Family stuff.'

Manny looked disappointed, 'But I thought you might want to join the swim disco?' he said. 'I'm leading it.' He took off his bathrobe and strode towards the pool.

'Another time,' said Tulip apologetically.

Ali kicked her. 'Or never,' she called cheerfully. 'We've got an awful fear of water. Terrified of the stuff. It's why we barely wash.'

'That was an unnecessary lie,' said Tulip.

'Totes necessary,' said Ali. 'They'd spot we're not boys if we were in a pool.'

'You're so right. You're not just a pretty face,'

Tulip grinned.

'Hah! Not even,' said Ali. 'And the last person to call me pretty got atomic-wedgied.'

'I was saying it ironically,' sighed Tulip. ''Cause, you know, we've got the exact same face.'

Manny was calling out to the elderly folks enthusiastically, and started playing some 80s workout music, with lots of synthesizers. His oversized vest flapped about with his baggy shorts, and Tulip noticed that both his clavicles were clear of tattoos, although he had a fair few on his arms and legs.

'I'm not absolutely sure that he's the bad guy,' she said. Nan-Nan had mentioned suspicious cash injections to this place. But if Manny had illegal money he was hiding it pretty well, most insanely wealthy criminals didn't do swim disco for the elderly in faded shorts.

Ali was looking into the main building. Catty was standing there, at a window, staring crossly at Witch, who was preening on the lawn with her new kitty entourage, taking over the battered croquet hoops as scratching posts. She clearly didn't like cats any more than she liked kids. Witch twisted and stared back at Catty, hissing with claws flared like she was ready to pounce at the glass. Catty decisively tugged the curtain shut.

'Nope, she's the bad guy,' said Ali. 'Don't know how or why yet, but just got a hunch. Manny's Mumsy is in this up to her drag-queen foundation line.'

CHAPTER 11:
WHAT TWITCH SAW

'Where are you going?' said Tulip, as Ali ran around the building.

'I'm gonna tail that woman, go through her room, you know, usual detective-invasion-of-privacy stuff,' said Ali. 'Find evidence. Fake wills. Big gold bathtubs of stolen cash.'

'We've got a message from Nan-Nan,' said Tulip, waving her phone at Ali. 'Remember?'

Ali rolled her eyes. 'Argh! Thought she was just picking up the boys. She doesn't need to live-tweet us her hilarious observations around the motorway ring-road.'

'You remember why she's picking up the boys?' said Tulip. 'Their dad? Stabbed.'

'Yeah, sure,' shrugged Ali. 'Don't you?'

'Wow,' said Tulip, sitting down behind the bushes and plugging in her headphones. 'When you fell out the empathy tree you really didn't hit a single branch on the way down.'

'Hey!' said Ali, grabbing an ear bud. 'Some of us deal with stuff differently. You get all aww and moochy, and I get stuff done!'

She flopped down next to Tulip, and saw a terse message from Nan-Nan, with a video link. It just said, 'Of interest.'

'You think there's any chance she sent us pictures of cute baby owls, or puppies that look like pastries?' asked Tulip.

'Sorry, dude,' said Ali, 'google them later.'

They played the link. The black and white film showed a view of their street, like security camera footage, from their window. Nothing weird there. Nan-Nan had their place wired from all angles. She usually used the creepy dolls on the high shelves that no one wanted to touch. But then the image started moving. It was like the camera was bouncing along down the stairs.

'Ugh, the doll's alive!' said Ali. 'I knew it!

Any doll with eyelids is bad news.'

'I once thought I heard them whispering to each other,' admitted Tulip. 'And then I woke up. But they were STILL whispering.' She looked accusingly at her twin.

'What! That was funny,' said Ali. 'It was a prank! It wasn't like I was whispering anything scary . . .'

'You said blood, blood, blood,' said Tulip flatly.

'I was giving you an idea for your blog,' said Ali. 'Red blood cells, and white blood cells. Haematology has been way too neglected.'

'You know what rhymes with haematology,' said Tulip. 'Apology.'

CHECK PAGE 303 OF THE APPENDIX FOR THE MINI-MEDIX BLOG POST
TWINTERMISSION! BLOOD FLOOD: RED, WHITE, AND PLATELET
OR THE QUICK GUIDE TO HAEMATOLOGY IN YOUR BIOLOGY

'Like in the lamest rap song ever,' said Ali. 'Look, creepy living doll's staring at the back door.'

She was right. The camera image had stalled on the make-shift cat flap the twins had fashioned by accident, when they had smashed one of the lower panes of glass in the French door, playing rolling chair hockey. Witchy had started using it to get in and out of the house, so their mum had put duct tape around the edges, with the lid of an old doughnut box as the flap.

'Great, even the haunted dolls are passive-aggressively critiquing our home improvements,' said Tulip. She knew it was silly to mind about the hole in the kitchen ceiling, which they'd caused by playing Flood Versus Waterfall in the bath during The Plunger Games, or the broken pane, but sometimes she was glad they didn't often have people around the house. She was embarrassed that their home wasn't a bit more normal. That *they* weren't a bit more normal.

'Pretty sure Creep-Doll is admiring our handiwork and initiative,' said Ali, who for once didn't sound sarcastic. 'Home-made-instant-cat-flap!' She really thought that everything she did was amazing.

'Must be great to be you,' said Tulip. She didn't sound sarcastic either, and Ali looked at her in surprise. But then she spotted something on the video, and paused it.

'Check it out!' There was a reflection in the plastic of the doughnut box. The camera wasn't one of the creepy blinky dolls. Of course it wasn't. It was Twitch, the Robo-Cat version of Witch, who they'd left hanging about their house.

'You know what,' said Tulip, 'why didn't Nan-Nan just take Twitch with us, if she needed a cat for the Cattery cover story? She'd have been better behaved.' She nodded towards Witch, who was now smugly licking her private parts in full view of some residents who were trying to eat their biscuits and drink their tea.

'Dinner and a show,' commented Ali. 'But I guess that our Witch can't do this.' She tapped the screen, as Twitch bounded through the doughnut-box-flap, and into the garden.

'She's giving us the visuals,' agreed Tulip, 'but what's she seen?'

They saw a moment later. There was a tall woman outside their house, in a fedora and trench coat, with a wild curly mop of hair trailing under the hat. She swished her coat, and was walking away, staring at something on her phone.

'That's not . . . Nan-Nan, is it?' said Tulip.

'Nope, it's not Nan-Nan,' said Ali, checking the time on the video. It wasn't that long ago. Nan-Nan had been with them.

'But she's definitely SWAT, right?' said Tulip. 'It would make sense to have one of the agents checking on the house.'

'She could be, but I can't tell which one in the black and white video,' said Ali. 'Those ladies rely WAY too much on their hair colour to tell them apart.'

'So why is she abandoning her post?' asked Tulip.

'I guess Twitch is gonna find out,' said Ali, as they watched the image bounce along the pavement.

The woman glanced behind her, and seeing the cat, got weirdly agitated. 'Shoo!' she hissed. And then she started running. With surprising athleticism.

Twitch couldn't keep up on the ground, but leapt up into a tree. And then along the rooftops. They could see the woman turn around and, satisfied that the cat wasn't following her, she slowed to a stroll and turned down a residential street.

'Hold on,' said Tulip, 'isn't that . . . the boys' street?'

'And that's the boys' house,' nodded Ali, as the woman stopped opposite a picture-pretty cottage, with a rose arch over the gate and a mural of trailing flowers and butterflies painted on the front wall. They saw the woman slip behind the large plane tree that was bursting out of the opposite pavement. Twitch leapt down, and sat next to the wall like a stone doorstop.

A car came down the quiet street.

'That's Wiggie,' said Tulip, 'so it's before the stabbing. Must be coming back from visiting the boys' mum in the hospital.'

'Look, he's giving Mum a ride,' added Ali. She'd spotted the big box of doughnuts in the passenger seat before she'd spotted her mum. She was gesticulating extravagantly with a doughnut that was sprinkling sugar all over her like fairy dust.

The Robo-Cat seemed to blink, and then audio switched on, too.

'You sure you don't want a cuppa, Minnie?' Wiggie was saying, as he jumped out of the car.

'Hot chocolate?' said Mum, hopefully,

clambering out herself, balancing the doughnut box.

'Oh, um,' said Wiggie, 'think I've got some carob. Could maybe mix that with almond milk?'

'Oh, no worries,' said Mum, hastily. 'See you tomorrow at the hospital. Give my love to your brave boys,' and she gave him a big hug, covering him in a cloud of sugar, too. She was waving to the window, Tulip guessed the boys were there, waiting. She strolled off towards home.

'Are you sure I can't drop you off?' he called after her.

'I have to finish off, I mean, work off the doughnuts,' called back Mum, as she turned the corner. Her shoulders shuddered.

'It's funny how you can see Mum think,' said Tulip. 'That shoulder shudder, that was deffo her thinking, *What weirdo would make hot choc with carob?*'

'That'll give her nightmares,' agreed Ali.

Wiggie stood sadly by himself for a moment. Dusting off the sugar.

'What's wrong with him?' said Ali, impatiently. Tapping the screen. 'Why isn't he going in?'

'I get it,' said Tulip. 'He doesn't want to go in. He doesn't know what he's going to say to the boys. About their mum.'

'Oh,' said Ali.

Wiggie was putting his proper face back on when a little old lady approached him, with a hideous feathered hat, hunched over and limping on a cane.

'No! Where'd she pop up from?' said Ali, fearfully.

Twitch seemed to think the same thing, and scanned up and down the street. No other cars, no open door. They couldn't tell if the tall trench coat woman was still concealed behind the tree.

'What can I do for you, madam?' he said brightly, smoothing out his sad expression with a helpful smile.

'More, what I can do for you, young man,' said the little old lady, in a rasping voice. She seemed wrapped in layers and layers of clothes. The girls couldn't believe that she was back. They couldn't believe that she was going to do it again.

'Where's that SWAT agent?' shrieked Tulip. 'It's her job to save the day, right?'

'Chillax,' said Ali, 'she's just making an entrance.'

But then the old lady lifted her cane, and from the cat's eye view, they saw the shining blade at the end of the stick.

'And I can DO FOR YOU . . .' she hissed, bringing down the cane.

'What?' asked Wiggie, confused.

'OMG, NO!' shrieked Tulip and Ali.

'NO!' shrieked two voices on the video feed, and they saw Jay and Zac bowling out of the house, already in their pyjamas. 'Help! Help!'

Mum was racing back around the corner. What she saw made her drop the box of doughnuts and run down the street. 'Call an ambulance,' she yelled.

People were pouring out of the houses, and surrounding Wiggie, the twins couldn't see him. He was on the ground.

Twitch looked down at the pavement, and now all the girls could see was sticky blood sinking into the sparkling grey stone. The cat's eye camera went back across the street, where the shadowy SWAT agent had been waiting. At least, the woman they had thought was the SWAT agent. She wasn't there. All that was there, puddled by the roots of the plane tree, was a trench coat. And a fedora hat.

There was a beep. Rapid text, END OF TRANSMISSION. And then the video stopped. And then they just saw Nan-Nan's terse message again.

Of interest.

CHAPTER 12:
DESSERT TROLLEY

The girls just stared at the phone. And then at each other.

'Of interest,' said Ali, eventually, into the silence. 'Nan-Nan really knows how to bury the big news.'

'Can't believe the boys were that stupid,' said Tulip, unexpectedly.

'Not to have spotted the nutty crone, and come out sooner to stop her?' asked Ali.

'Nope, to have come out at all,' said Tulip. 'If someone's stabbing people in the street, you don't GO OUT towards them. You stay in and lock the door.'

'It's their dad,' said Ali simply. 'Don't really remember what it was like to have a dad. But I'd have done the same thing.'

Tulip smiled. 'That's sweet,' she said.

'That,' said Ali, 'is a horrible accusation. You take that back. I'm the smart one. You can be the sweet one.'

'As the smart one,' said Tulip, 'what would you say was happening in Twitch's video feed?'

'The person who attacked Wiggie looks an awful lot like the person who attacked Momo,' said Ali. 'But she's in disguise. A double disguise. Trench coat comes off and she's the bag lady stabber.'

'And in the trench coat, she's dressed a lot like someone from Nan-Nan's SWAT team,' said Tulip.

'And what do Momo and Wiggie have in common?' said Ali. 'Momo's a social worker student who moonlights in the service industries. And Wiggie's a gluten-free, dairy-free, stay-at-home dad.'

'Mum,' said Tulip. 'They're both friends with Mum.'

'So . . . Nan-Nan's SWAT team is taking out

Mum's mates?' said Ali. 'That's insane.'

'OMG,' said Tulip. 'Someone in the SWAT team's gone ROGUE!' she looked wildly around.

'Don't know why you're so surprised,' commented Ali. 'Nan-Nan's friends swing around in the woods in matching outfits with vigilante moves. 'Course they be crazy.'

'And now they've set us up here. And they've got Nan-Nan to leave us ALONE. Abandoned!' shuddered Tulip. 'With a memory-wiped guy back from the dead who hated us.'

'Oh, that guy,' scoffed Ali. 'We can take him. There's two of us, and he doesn't even know who we are. Heck, he doesn't even know who HE is!'

They were surprised by a shadowy figure in dark robes rising up behind them.

'Who doesn't know who he is?' said Manny, tightening the belt on his towelling bathrobe.

'Couldn't you cough or something?' said Ali. 'Creeping up on people with cat-like stealth is NOT cool.'

'Oh, is hiding in bushes cool?' said Manny, with interest. 'Like I said, I'm not very down with the kids.'

'You really gotta lose that catchphrase,' said Tulip.

Manny was still in his water-disco gear, his robe flapping about his skinny legs like some crazed Arthur Dent in search of a towel. He needed one, as his hair was dripping. There was a jagged scar across the back of his head, his damp hair parted on either side of it.

'That looks painful,' said Tulip.

'What?' he said. 'Oh that. Had it for ages. Mumsy says my brother hit me on the head with a shovel when I was little.'

'Really?' said Ali, frowning at Tulip. The scar didn't look old. It was still pretty red and raw.

'Really,' said Manny. 'You must know what brothers are like.'

'Nah, not really,' said Tulip, before Ali gave her a you're-stupid stare, and hit her on the back of the head. 'I mean, really, just like that. Totally. I've totally got a brother.'

'Can we help you with anything?' said Ali, pointedly. 'I mean, we're kinda busy, being moody kids and all, and if I've missed an important text in the last sixty seconds I'm gonna get pretty cross . . .'

'Must be nice to have so many friends,' said Manny, 'that you've got someone sending you messages every minute.'

'It is,' said Ali, 'it really is,' and as if on cue, her phone started beeping. So did Tulip's. Manny looked a bit wistful.

'Sorry. Just wanted to tell you that grub's up,' he said, 'and the good stuff goes fast.'

'Not sure I wanna eat anything in this place that doesn't come in sealed packets,' said Tulip in a low voice. 'Let's go back to the room.'

'You're kidding, dude,' said Ali. 'The room only has one entrance and exit. It's basically a trap. You wanna walk into a trap? Like the dumb kid who follows the moaning voice into the basement when they should be walking out the door.'

'Well, we should hide, or something,' said Tulip. 'The vid's a warning. This place isn't safe. Catty's super-creepy and we might have been set up by a rogue SWAT who's attacking Mum's contacts! Nan-Nan's sooo irresponsible leaving us here.'

'It's a bit safer than being on the front doorstep was for Wiggie,' pointed out Ali. 'And the best place to hide is in a crowd.' She nodded towards the elderly people shuffling with enthusiasm towards the tatty barn extension. It had a 'Dining Room' sign written over it in a jolly script, with a picture of Garfield slouching over a lasagne.

'Ugh, that cat's so smug,' said Tulip, 'and so unoriginal. He literally just leans into the trope of being a fat, smug cat.'

'YOUR cat's fat and smug,' said Ali, pointing to Witch who was slinking into the scrum. She obviously smelled food, too.

'Now she's *my* cat?' muttered Tulip, following Ali. 'Fine, let's hide in plain sight.'

'Finally,' said Ali, over her shoulder.

'You're just hungry, right?' added Tulip.

'So hungry,' said Ali. 'I'd eat any adorable woodland animal around here if it was fried and served with ketchup.'

'So, I don't think you need to worry about not getting stuff in packets,' said Ali, looking down the long trestle tables.

The dining room was set out like a school hall, with stackable plastic chairs, the sort they had in fast food restaurants with a twenty-minute maximum before your bum got numb with discomfort. They saw the old dears sitting down and rubbing their hands with genuine glee as trays with packets of crisps, crackers, cheese, sausage rolls, marshmallows, biscuits and cake slices were dumped on the tables by the two lurch-like henchmen, Greasy and Frankenstein, who'd trapped the twins earlier.

The guests were taking a while to settle down, mainly because they seemed to have so much kit with them to untangle and set up. There were portable oxygen cannisters on wheels, drips hanging from drip stands, and walking frames and wheelchairs.

'Ugh, it's like being in the hospital canteen,' said Ali. 'Full of sicky-icky people.'

'But everything's in plastic packets,' said Tulip, in a sort of wonder. 'It's more like a kid's birthday party at a scooter park.'

'Hey,' said Ali, to one of the henchmen. 'Talking to you, interchangeable dudes. What is this stuff?'

'Dinner,' shrugged the Greasy guy.

'It's also breakfast, lunch and tea,' said Frankenstein. 'I was worried about the plastic packaging, but we only buy stuff that's out of date, so by using it, instead of binning it, we're actually saving the planet's resources.' He opened his jacket, and showed his 'I heart the environment' T-shirt. He tapped his chest with his fist.

'Wow, out of date stuff from the discount stores for your guests, you're all heart,' agreed Ali.

'You being sarcastic?' asked Tulip.

'I really don't know,' said Ali, grabbing a chair and seating herself between two oxygen cannisters, and knocking over a wobbling drip stand. 'But Manny's right, the good stuff goes fast! That old cow down the end is hoarding all the marshmallow wafer sandwiches!'

'But where's the protein?' said Tulip. 'The vitamins! The vegetables! The fruit!'

'Here you are, love,' said a lady in a wildly patterned headscarf, with a lot of chunky jewellery. She was smoking through her tracheostomy in her throat, and she threw over a packet of puffy-shaped sweets. 'They're orange.'

'Orange is definitely a fruit,' said Ali. 'She's got you there.' She waved to the lady, 'Hey, sugar, pass me some sugar!'

The lady grinned toothlessly, and threw another packet her way.

'So, what's your deal?' Ali asked her.

'Oh, I'm married, dear,' said the lady. 'I'm flattered you asked though.'

'What! Yuk!' said Ali. 'No, I meant what's going on with that?' and she waved to the hole in the lady's throat. 'Smoking kills.'

CHECK PAGE 305 OF THE APPENDIX FOR THE MINI-MEDIX BLOG POST TWINTERVENTION! SMOKING ISN'T SMART OR WHAT YOU DO WHEN SOMEONE'S BLOWING SMOKE!

'Oh, I KNOW that, dear,' said the lady. 'I'm about a billion years old. And not bothered about extending my longevity. It's too late for that. Already pushing up the daisies. One foot in the grave. Knock-knock-knocking on heaven's door . . .'

'So that's not very positive,' said Tulip. 'Old age isn't an ILLNESS. Our Nan-Nan says that she'd rather get old than the alternative.'

'Yeah, you're not really helping yourself with the little white death sticks,' said Ali.

'Judgey children, well that's refreshing,' huffed the lady. 'Of course old age isn't an illness. ILLNESS is an illness. I've got so many comorbidities it's like a Christmas list from A for Arthritis to Z for . . .'

'You're depressing us, Doris,' said LeRoi the board game hustler, who had just wandered in. He was already inhaling junk food by the mouthful, as he took a seat next to her. 'You're putting me off my packaged meat-substitute snack.' He held up a package which said 'Mr Meaty Meatballs! May contain meat.'

'Ooh, gimme,' said Ali, 'I wanna try! Our mum won't let us have those, and she eats almost anything.'

'She's right, they're carcinogenic,' said Doris, eating one herself.

'Yeah, ship's sailed on that,' said LeRoi. 'Can I pass you anything, young sir?' He winked at Tulip.

'Um, yeah, the Monster Munch and the chocolate-covered cake slices. Oh, and the mini Mars Bars,' said Tulip. She piled them up into a satisfying pyramid, and peering over it, asked, 'Can I save some meatballs for our cat, Witch? She's gone feral, been hunting the wildlife since we got here.'

'Not sure I'd feed those ones to a cat,' said LeRoi doubtfully. 'Too many additives.'

'Yep, the salt and potassium would probably

give Witch a heart attack,' agreed Ali.

'Happens to us all,' cackled Doris, 'with a bit of a shock! You seen the 'special dessert' trolley over there?'

'That's a crash cart,' said Tulip, spotting the trolley. It had a defibrillator on it, and a breathing mask. 'For when people have a cardiac arrest.'

'Didn't think hotels had those as standard,' frowned Ali, looking at the guests uneasily. 'Does that happen a lot around here?'

'I've had the paddles twice,' said Doris. 'But we don't have kitty-sized ones, so best let your cat here hunt down the sky-rats. Oh, and the rat-rats,' she added. 'That would be helpful. We've enough of them round here.'

'You know, a cat-friendly hotel really oughta have cat food,' pointed out Ali, critically.

'Do you really think this is just a hotel?' said one sweet-looking woman, her hair a halo of frizz. She looked urgently at the others. 'Their granny hasn't told them! They can't know her prognosis.'

'Told us what?' said Ali. 'What prognosis?'

'We've said too much, dear,' said Doris, getting up hastily. 'Enjoy the emulsified fats and additives.'

'Back at ya, Doris,' said Tulip, looking after her in confusion.

'Not so fast, Doris!' said Ali. 'You can never say too much! What's the low-down?'

'Bossy kids,' huffed Doris, 'just as refreshing,' and she transferred to her wheelchair and rolled off.

'Awkward. Could I have some Wotsits?' asked LeRoi.

Tulip offered them to him politely.

'Uh-thank-you-very-much,' said LeRoi, in a sort of Elvis impersonation, accepting them. 'LeRoi means the King in French,' he explained. 'I got the nickname for my legendary Elvis karaoke.'

'Hah, rubbish impression,' said Ali.

'I won AWARDS for it. And it's better than your boy impression, little lady,' commented LeRoi.

'What!' said Ali. 'What gave it away?'

'You crossed your legs,' said LeRoi. 'Dead giveaway. And you've got about a dozen other tells. I should know. I used to impersonate women professionally.'

'A female impersonator?' asked Tulip with

interest. 'So cool! Like in a show?'

'We were more of a troupe,' said LeRoi. 'Had a flair for the dramatic. Liked to make a big entrance. And an even BIGGER exit.' He grinned and with a sweeping full-arc-air-guitar strum followed by another 'Uh-thank-you-very-much', with extra geriatric-swivel, he wandered off.

CHAPTER 13:
BAT-NAN'S SIGNAL

Ali and Tulip were left with a gap around them, and a pile of the least desirable junk food. Most of it had bright foreign labels in unrecognizable alphabets. There was one package of sausage-type stuff which was just called 'So-Sausagey'. Ali inspected it, unsure if the lack of specification was admirable or deeply worrying.

'You worried about which animal is in that?' asked Tulip, perceptively. 'Or which bit of the animal?'

'Both,' admitted Ali, putting down the packet. 'Could be bunny guts or dog ears for all we know.' She ripped open a different one, with marshmallows sandwiched between wafers and sprinkles.

'D'you think there are more rogue SWAT agents lurking around here?' asked Tulip, looking around nervously.

'Honestly, who could tell?' said Ali, checking her phone again. Nothing from Nan-Nan. 'I can literally only tell them apart by their wigs. Like reality TV contestants and hair extensions.'

'Yeah, without their costume, they could be ANYONE here,' said Tulip. 'Apart from the guys.'

'They could even be guys,' argued Ali. 'We're being boys. We're like the ONLY boys here.'

And then, the door of the dining room swung open. And Ali and Tulip blinked and looked, as standing there in the frame, with the light behind them, were Zac and Jay.

'Not any more,' said Tulip, jumping up delightedly.

They were still in their pyjamas, Ali noticed. Slightly bloodstained. Probably whatever they'd been wearing when they ran out to their dad. And Zac was holding a ratty old teddy with ears chewed off to triangles, like a cat's.

'Nah, I stand by my original statement,' sniffed Ali, but she stood up too, and waved them over.

'Come on, grab seats for the eats!' she called.

'We were so worried about you,' said Tulip, hugging them.

Zac returned her hug, gratefully. Jay stood a bit more stiffly.

'Yup, that's how I show I'm worried about people,' he said, looking at the junk food mountain. 'Have a tea party and eat empty calories.'

'Aw, you must really care,' said Zac, taking a seat. 'No one would eat this stuff willingly.' He looked around, and asked in a low voice, 'Did you see it? The video from the Robo-Cat?'

The girls nodded.

'How's your dad?' asked Tulip.

'He'll be OK,' said Zac. 'He's in the hospital. They got a police guard on him AND Momo now.'

'And how are you?' asked Ali, unexpectedly.

Tulip beamed at her approvingly.

'Well, we're here, with you,' said Jay, looking around with distaste. 'We're tickety-boo.'

'Yeah it's kind of a dump and that kind of

sucks,' agreed Ali, offering him a packet of popcorn.

He shrugged and took it.

'At least it's gluten free,' he said. 'I can cling to that small crumb of comfort.'

'Where's Nan-Nan?' said Tulip, looking around. 'Didn't she bring you?'

'She said something about getting back into costume,' said Zac. 'Is there a dress rehearsal or something happening here?' He looked around, less critically than Jay. 'Funny place to put a nursing home.' He carried on, 'I mean, there's wheelchair access, and some basic medical facilities, but there aren't nearly enough staff on duty.'

'What did you say?' asked Ali.

'Staff,' said Zac, picking up the So-Sausagey packet, and shuddering as he put it back down again. Just as Mum had shuddered on the video when Wiggie had suggested using carob for hot chocolate.

'Before that,' said Tulip.

'Nursing home,' said Zac. 'Unless, it's not a hospice, is it?'

Ali slapped Tulip's forehead. 'Duh!' she said. 'Nursing home!'

'Slash-hospice?' said Tulip, whacking her back. 'That's what that lady meant by prognosis. NOT a hotel. This place is for poorly people.'

'You didn't know?' said Zac. 'How could you not spot that? You're not THAT self-obsessed.'

'I guess seeing sick people is kind of normal for us,' mused Tulip, 'with all the hanging out at the hospital.'

'And we were distracted by a SERIOUS series plot twist,' snapped Ali defensively. 'There's a returning villain from the dead.'

'As I keep saying, you lack basic observation skills,' said Jay. He started glumly eating rice crackers, the plainest thing on the table. 'And you're meant to slap your OWN forehead when you come to some giddy conclusion.'

'Except we're basically the same person,' said Tulip.

'Yeah, there's two of me,' agreed Ali.

'You? No, there's two of ME,' said Tulip. 'We're not having the sidekick conversation again.'

'*Anyway*, your nan said to wait for the signal,' said Zac. 'She said you'd know what she meant.'

Catty, the scary over-made-up cat-hating kid-hating woman came into the dining hall, and the casual patter and chatter halted. Manny trailed in behind her, still in his towelling robe.

'Wait a minute,' said Jay, jumping up, his eyes popping out at the sight of Manny, 'isn't that . . .'

'Long story,' said Ali, tugging him down. 'You see what I mean about the distracting twist?' And she slapped down Zac's hand, as he was gaping and pointing, too. 'Be subtle. And be cool! We'll catch you up later.'

'Fine. But who's the Trunchbull?' asked Zac.

'She's Catty, Manny's Monster Mumsy,' said Ali. 'Proprietor of Catty's Cattery. And proprietor means owner . . .'

'I know! Don't girlsplain,' huffed Jay.

'Shush, dears,' said Doris, rolling back towards them, pushed by LeRoi. 'Catty doesn't like interruptions. It's speech time.'

'Dear guests,' said Catty, at the head of the dining hall, and Manny bowed his head, as solemnly as though they were about to pray.

'We'd like to remember those we lost this week,' said Catty. 'Our friends, our benefactors, whose generous donations have made it possible to keep Catty's Cattery running, not for our profit, dear friends, no, for yours.' Her beaming tooth-stuffed smile was like a strobe light.

She held up a bucket. 'Now, let's start the collection, and be thankful. Remember, we like the stuff that jingles. But we prefer the stuff that folds.'

'Hey, that's my line,' whispered Ali. 'She's been nicking my material.'

'HashtagCattyCares,' said one of the old folks at the head of the table, looking besottedly at Catty.

'Like, share, and subscribe,' nodded his partner, patting his hand affectionately.

'Thank you, Hamish and Romesh,' said Catty. 'But you know we don't encourage mentions of Catty's Cattery on social media. It's our *little secret*.'

'Sooo creepy,' said Jay.

'Our secret *sanctuary*!' snapped Catty, glaring at the interruption. 'Now, who's going to start?'

Hamish and Romesh began slowly unrolling a wad of notes from their tweed-jacketed pockets. Catty watched them keenly, her eyes wide and bright, exaggerated in make-up that had basically outlined them like a kid's drawing.

Just then, the fire alarm went off.

A couple of moths came out of the sprinklers

above their heads.

And then there was a full-on explosion of water, gushing out with force as the old plumbing clanked into action, and shot off the sprinkler heads like weapons.

'Why do those even work?' screeched Catty desperately, shielding her rock-hard hair under her scarf.

'Um, I got them fixed, Mumsy,' said Manny. 'Thought it best. Health and safety for our guests . . .'

'Who cares about *their* health and safety,' she hissed. 'You know these people are dy—' A fresh jet of water hit her straight between the eyes. She shrieked and hid her face behind a paper plate shield.

'Sorry,' said Ali, holding up a broken gushing tube. 'Was trying to fix it.'

'Shouldn't there be an evacuation plan?' asked Zac politely, holding up his hand like he was at school.

Jay slapped it down in irritation.

'Seriously, dude,' he whispered, 'you're such a dope.'

'Aw,' said Zac, 'you really think I'm dope?'

'Yes,' said Tulip fiercely, daring Jay to

contradict her. 'He does.'

'Evacuation?' said Manny. He looked around desperately while everyone looked at him. Catty's made-up face was melting away, and she ran off whimpering.

'Um, calm down, everyone. So who's the fire thingummy?' Manny called out.

'That would be you, dear,' shouted Doris, helpfully.

'Viva las Vegas!' shouted LeRoi, much less helpfully, with an extended air-guitar solo and hip swivel. A few people around him groaned and rolled their eyes.

'Right, well, follow me,' said Manny, 'to the evacuation thingummy.' He marched off with his robe flapping around his tattooed calves, leaving frantic mayhem behind him. Everyone was torn between saving their snacks from a soggy fate and getting out through the scrum.

'I knew it,' said Doris, trying to light another cigarette in the downpour. 'The snacks had a longer sell-by-date than us.'

'You're not going to expire just yet,' said LeRoi, pushing her out of the hall.

Meanwhile Ali and Tulip were calmly checking their phones.

'Quit Insta-geeking,' said Zac, looking alarmed. 'We've gotta get out.'

'You got it?' said Tulip urgently to Ali.

Ali nodded, and sighed when a soaked Witch leapt up in her arms. Her timid kitty followers were more sensibly sheltering under the trestle tables or shooting outside between people's ankles. 'Wow, you're hideous when wet,' she said to the cat. 'Wet cat is like the worst smell ever.'

'Got what?' said Zac.

'Guessing that was the signal,' said Jay, nodding towards the fire alarm. 'Your nan's not too subtle, is she?'

'The Bat-Nan signal. Could've been worse,' shrugged Ali. 'She could've actually set the place on fire. In fact I wouldn't put it past her.'

'She's messaged us to meet back in the woods,' said Tulip. 'Let's go.'

'We literally just got here,' complained Jay.

'Hey! Less squawking, more walking,' said Ali, chucking an open packet of crisps at him. He caught them clumsily at his chest, and they exploded all over him.

'Your hand-eye coordination sucks,' she said pleasantly. 'You gotta work on that.'

'He's more the computer guy who eats organic snacks on the sofa,' said Zac, plucking a crisp expertly from the air and eating it. 'Not the hand-eye coordination guy.'

'By the way,' said Jay, 'why are you two dressed like Dennis-the-Menace car-crashed into Bart Simpson and Horrid Henry?'

'I'm guessing they were Nan-Nan's only reference to how boys dress,' shrugged Tulip, looking down at herself.

'You're supposed to be boys?' said Jay. He stopped, and his mouth twisted.

'What?' said Ali and Tulip.

'Just give me a moment,' he said. 'I'm too sad about Dad to laugh out loud. I'm laughing in my head.'

Ali grabbed him by the pyjama collar and frogmarched him out.

CHAPTER 14:
EVIL TWINS

Nan-Nan rolled out of the woods looking like her old self. Leather-jacketed with her black and silver hair rolling back in waves. But she was already costume changing in front of them into the helpless old granny she'd presented to the Cattery goons, flapping out the flowery dress.

'So, what's the intel?' she asked briskly.

'No intel,' said Ali innocently. 'We just stayed in our room, like you said.'

There was a heavy pause, with Ali and Nan-Nan staring at each other. Then they both burst out laughing, back-slapping each other.

'Hahaha,' said Nan-Nan. 'It's sweet that you think I'd believe that.'

'Why did you even tell us to stay in our rooms?' said Tulip, looking annoyed with both of them.

'Plausible deniability,' said Nan-Nan promptly.

'What does that mean?' asked Zac. He was a bit in awe of Nan-Nan.

'It means that if anything happened to these toxic little twins, it's not because of my lousy grandparenting,' said Nan-Nan. 'It's because they didn't do what they were told. Not my bad.'

'Well, first bit of intel,' said Tulip, 'we don't know if Manny actually is Sprotland. Looks like him, but he doesn't know us, and barely knows himself. And he's actually quite nice. And the guy we knew was a bit of a jerk.'

'He definitely DID have a BIG knock on the head,' said Ali, 'we saw the scar.'

'Hmm,' said Jay, 'I heard that a knock on the head could cause a complete personality change. There was that one about the nutty surgeon who started burning his initials into patients' livers, when he was operating.'

'Aww, that was from my blog, on Monstrous Medics,' beamed Tulip.

'Might've been checking in on it,' admitted Jay.

'Mainly to check if *he's* in on it,' grinned Zac. 'He's got a thing about his privacy being invaded by your blogging. Ever since you told the world about his allergies.'

'You two are literally the only subscribers,' said Tulip. 'I've got more followers on my fake Instagram about Witch. It's called Witch Around the World.'

'You've got a catstagram?' said Zac. 'Awesome!'

'Ali follows it,' said Tulip, showing Jay and Zac on her phone. 'Look, she commented on the one where I photoshopped Witch in front of the Pyramids.'

'That's her comment?' said Jay. 'It just says, "*Hahaha so lame.*"'

'And I meant it,' said Ali, sincerely.

Tulip sighed, and tapped the front of her head. 'If you actually read the science bits of my blog,' she said, 'you'd see that the frontal cortex is the bit that has to be bashed to change the personality. Manny's scar is on the occipital area, at the back.'

CHECK PAGE 307 OF THE APPENDIX FOR THE
MINI-MEDIX BLOG POST
TWINTERMISSION: MINI GUIDE TO THE BITS OF
YOUR BRAIN
OR WHAT HAPPENS WHEN YOU GET A WHACK TO
YOUR HEAD!

'And we couldn't see that tattoo which he had done on his clavicle,' she said, patting her own collarbone. 'Unless he camouflaged it with some slap he stole from Catty, who is apparently his mother.'

'Seriously,' sniggered Ali, 'her face started melting like wax when you hit the sprinklers.' She demonstrated with her fingers rippling down her face. 'Literally, if you want a portrait of that lady, just grab her pillowcase, it'll all be printed on there.'

'Poor thing,' said Tulip. 'She might wear all that make-up because she's horribly scarred. Or lost her nose or something.'

'His mother,' said Nan-Nan, her eyebrows hitting her hairline. 'He's got a MOTHER! That's very fishy.'

'Yeah, come to think of it, Sprotland didn't have any family, did he?' said Tulip. 'I mean, no one came to his funeral.'

'So if that's really him, he's become a massive amnesiac suggestible blob,' said Ali, 'and he's being royally manipulated by someone.'

'Couldn't happen to a nicer man,' sniffed Nan-Nan.

She'd finished changing. 'Will I do?' She struck a pose in the enormous dress and pastel cardigan, putting on her helpless-little-lady voice.

'Nobody would say *I do* to that,' laughed Ali. 'You look like a picture of someone selling cookies on a biscuit box.'

'Um,' said Zac, 'you know, nice outfit, but we're still in our pyjamas.'

'Oh,' said Nan-Nan. 'Maybe borrow some spare stuff from the girls.'

'You mean, wear the girls' clothes?' asked Jay, mortified. 'Not funny.'

'Ha!' said Ali. 'Too funny. Two sets of cross-dressing twins.'

'Positively Shakespearean,' said Nan-Nan. 'It'll set the scene for some hilarious misunderstandings.'

'Unless,' said Tulip, slowly. Her eyes were widening. She had that lightbulb-over-the-head look of sudden inspiration.

'What?' said Zac, politely.

'Unless, Sprotland had a twin!' She blurted it out, and jumped up and down with excitement. 'That's it! He has a NON-evil twin!'

'Why does there always have to be an evil twin?' complained Ali. 'We get a bad enough press already with the creepy secret language and stuff.'

'There doesn't *have* to be an evil twin,' said Jay, looking meaningfully at her. 'It's just that there is.'

'Hah!' said Ali. 'Back at ya.'

'Hey, I'm not evil,' said Jay, seriously stung. 'I'm polite and punctual and . . .'

'Punchable?' said Ali, pretending to mishear, aiming for his shoulder.

Nan-Nan rapped the edge of her wheelchair, sharply. 'A non-evil twin?' She nodded at Tulip. 'Well, that's very provable, go get us some of Manny's DNA.'

'On it,' said Tulip, nudging Ali.

'And what about us?' said Zac, tugging Jay reluctantly towards Nan-Nan. 'We wanna help.'

'Are you sure?' said Nan-Nan. 'I'm just meant to be babysitting you boys. Not making you work the case.'

'We want to help,' repeated Zac with determination. He raised his chin. 'We can't just sit around. We need to be useful.'

'But boys?' said Nan-Nan. 'I really don't work with boys. Just because . . . well, you know . . .'

'You know . . . what, Nan-Nan? Slugs and snails and puppy dog tails?' said Ali sarcastically. 'Is that what little boys are made of?'

'Yeah, you're sounding kind of bigoted, Nan-Nan,' Tulip admitted, uncomfortably. 'I mean, what would you say if someone said they wouldn't work with Mum, just because she was a girl?'

'Someone did say that,' said Nan-Nan. 'And I slapped them around their big stupid, stupid face. Got into all sorts of trouble with it. Apparently hitting the four-year-old's karate teacher is frowned upon.'

'Her karate teacher?' repeated Zac, sure he had misunderstood.

'Black belt,' said Nan-Nan, cheerfully. 'His fault for turning her away from the class. He cried buckets. Such silly rules, they had those days. I had to pretend I'd had an epileptic fit, to get away with it.'

Zac and Jay were watching Nan-Nan with eyes like dinner plates. They didn't know her well enough to know that she probably wasn't joking.

'It's fine,' said Jay. 'Don't worry about us helping with the case, we'll just stay with you.' He added a bit uncertainly, 'You do know that babysitting doesn't involve sitting on actual babies, right?'

'Yeah, I'm looking forward to it,' said Zac slyly. 'We can sit and have a really long conversation about your life. You can tell us all about the old country.'

Nan-Nan looked discomfited. 'What old country? I forget which one.'

'And the war,' said Jay. 'Tell us ALL about the war. Where you lost your legs.'

'I've forgotten which one of those it was, too,' said Nan-Nan.

'And you can tell them about our *grandfather*,' added Tulip. This was clearly a low blow. 'All about your *relationships*.'

'Relationships?' squealed Nan-Nan. 'I am

NOT talking about relationships. And I'm really not sure I remember which one was your grandfather. You know how quickly I get bored.'

'Or,' said Jay, 'we could help?'

'Fine!' snapped Nan-Nan. 'We'll investigate Manny's Mumsy while the girls get the biological samples.' She rolled into action, 'Spit-spot!'

Witch had been curled up next to Tulip, but seeing a free ride back to the house, leapt onto Nan-Nan's lap, making her look like an unconvincing Bond-villain-cat-lady.

'Never work with children or animals,' she muttered to herself. 'The SWAT team warned me.'

'Yeah, well the SWAT team don't know everything,' pointed out Tulip. 'Looks like one of them might've gone rogue. You saw that video.'

Nan-Nan rolled her eyes, just like Ali. 'First, whoever that wannabe woman was, she wasn't SWAT, not in those stupid smart shoes. SWAT girls wear *trainers* for a fast getaway. Second, they're ALL rogue agents, and so am I! That's how we ended up in the SWAT team. I wouldn't trust any of those girls as far as I could roll them.'

'Why do you work with people you don't

trust?' asked Zac, confused.

'Same reason I do anything,' said Nan-Nan, wheeling back towards the Cattery. 'For the fun of it.'

'I'm not sure I'm having fun,' said Zac.

'Maybe we're not doing it right,' said Jay, putting his arm around his shoulder.

CHAPTER 15:
MAGIC ACT

Nan-Nan got out of her wheelchair, and limped over the weedy grass on her fake legs, towards the fire-evacuation point, which seemed to be next to the pool. Manny was still there, inefficiently trying to do a headcount from everyone who had gathered there, but the soaked people kept wheeling or wandering around while they were chatting.

'Oh, for goodness sake, it's like herding kittens,' he complained.

'It's the Cattery,' laughed Doris. 'Of course it is.' She'd started vaping as all her cigarettes were wet.

'And I've lost the children,' he complained, flapping the guest register about in the air. 'There were two little boys.'

'Nope, there were four boys,' said LeRoi. 'I came back to the table and they'd doubled.'

'Think *you're* seeing double,' suggested Manny. 'You want to check your specs. There were definitely just two boys.'

'No, definitely four, dear,' said Doris. 'And I don't wear glasses.'

'Seriously?' said Manny. 'Good lord, the children are multiplying! Like bacteria. Why aren't they in the guest book?'

Tulip and Ali snuck up behind Manny. Ali tapped him on the shoulder. 'Hey, do you wanna see a magic trick?'

'There you are! Sure, I love magic,' he said, turning around. Tulip tried to tug a hair from his head as he did.

'Ouch!' he shrieked.

'Ooh, think you got bitten,' said Tulip, pretending to bat away a bug from his head.

'What's the magic trick?' said Manny.

Ali whispered something to him, and he grinned and nodded.

'Ladies and gentleman, we have an astonishing

magical spectacular for you!' he announced.

Everyone turned to stare at him. Ali gave a thumbs-up, while Nan-Nan and the boys hurried into the main building.

'If you remain still long enough for me to tick you off my list,' said Manny, 'I'll transport this young man here,' he pointed to Ali, 'over there!' And he pointed to a far-away picnic table, across the pool. It was draped with a plastic cloth, with metal weights clipped around the edge to keep it down.

He called out the names of the residents, and breathed a sigh of relief when everyone was accounted for and ticked off.

'So we're all alive and kicking,' called Doris. 'What about the magic?'

'No problem,' said Ali. She stood on a table and called out, 'DRUM ROLL, please!'

Doris and LeRoi obliged, drumming on their legs.

'And count to three!' Ali yelled. 'All together! One, two, THREE!' And the audience watched as the shouty boy, dressed like Dennis-the-Horrid-Bart-Henry, threw handfuls of crisps and sweets in the air, like confetti, and jumped down, disappearing under the plastic tablecloth.

There was a collective gasp. As at the exact same moment, he leapt UP onto the OTHER table. On the other side of the pool! And for dramatic effect, he burst a huge packet of crisps in the air, which scattered down gently to rest in the pool. And bowed.

'Ta-da!' said Manny, looking pleased with the massive round of applause and cheers. 'And that's magic!'

'Hurrah for Manny the Magician,' said Romesh and Hamish. 'HashtagMagicianManny,' said Romesh. 'Like, share, subscribe,' agreed Hamish.

'Um, OK,' said Manny, confused. 'Right, thanks for letting me do the headcount. I'm pretty sure there wasn't a fire. I'm going to go mop up the dining room.'

Ali had meanwhile crawled under the tables, and along the ground, to reach the table on the far side of the pool, where Tulip had been hiding, waiting for her cue to leap out on top of it. Once Tulip had finally finishing taking the bows she jumped back down to join her, under the tablecloth.

'Props for the thing you did with the bursting crisp packet,' Ali whispered to Tulip. 'Loving the showmanship.'

'It's still food,' said Tullip. 'I hate wasting stuff. But you did it first, so I thought I had to look just like you.'

'You did a good job,' grinned Ali. 'At looking just like me. Who knew?'

'Oh shush,' said Tulip. 'I'm gonna head inside. You stay here for a bit. If they see us together, it'll spoil the illusion.'

But before she left, she turned around, remembering what the point of the magic trick diversion had been. 'You got it, right?' asked Tulip.

Ali opened her fist, and showed a few hairs. 'Got them!' she said. 'Should be enough for Nan-Nan's lab team to do a DNA match. Just took them from the bathrobe, so it didn't even hurt him.'

'Thought you'd rip them right off his little beard,' joked Tulip.

But Ali just looked cross. 'You ever think,' said Ali, 'that I get enough of people thinking I'm some kinda pit bull?'

'Oh, people don't think that,' said Tulip.

'You're a rubbish liar,' said Ali. 'I don't care if other people think it. But I didn't think you thought it, too.' She jumped up. '*I'm* going first.'

She swanned off, in an obvious huff.

'What just happened?' said Tulip, to her departing back.

CHAPTER 16:
CATTY'S ROOM

They found Nan-Nan limping impatiently around their room, with the boys busily brushing their teeth after lunch. They were dressed in the girls' T-shirts and shorts.

'Don't say a word,' said Jay grumpily, tugging the too-short T-shirt down, even though the girls liked their clothes roomy. 'So many owls. And llamas.' He rinsed and spat in the sink.

'Better than the blood-stained pyjamas,' shrugged Zac, drying his own toothbrush carefully. 'And I like the hedgehogs. They're spiky.'

Ali looked at him in horror. 'Yeah, you can keep the clothes,' she said. 'I'll just burn them if you give them back to me.'

'Thanks,' said Zac. 'You guys wear a lot of blue and green. Like hospital scrubs.'

'I only wear black or dark grey,' said Nan-Nan.

''Cause you're the Bat-Nan,' joked Jay. 'Tulip told me that,' he added uncertainly, as though he suddenly realized he didn't know Nan-Nan well enough to joke with her.

'Well, that. And mainly because the blood shows up much less.' She looked down in disapproval at her floral dress.

'Any luck investigating Catty?' asked Ali.

Nan-Nan snorted. 'Hah! I wish. The princesses here took this long getting washed and changed.'

'Hey, firstly, thank you for comparing us to royalty,' said Jay. 'And secondly, that's really quick for us.' He held out his hands. 'We'd usually cut our nails and do our weekly nit-check, but we skipped that for you.'

'Yeah, there were definitely more nits in this place than we'd bring in,' agreed Zac.

Nan-Nan sighed, and pushed open the door.

'Right, let's go find Manny's Mumsy.'

Just then, a creaking door opened further along the corridor.

'I think you've found her,' said Catty, glaring down the hallway at Nan-Nan and Jay, who was standing behind her. The others instinctively remained behind their bedroom door.

Catty's extravagant scarf looped over her rock-hard hair and was wrapped around her throat. Her make-up had been re-done, and her eyebrows arched dramatically behind her oversized shades.

'And who exactly,' she said, looking at Nan-Nan leaning on her stick, 'are you?'

'I'm a new guest,' whimpered Nan-Nan, hiding under her own scarf, putting on her own shades.

The girls, hidden back in the room, looked round in shock. Nan-Nan sounded like a completely different person. Her voice was like a weak old lady, at death's door.

'I haven't got long to go, I'm afraid.' She coughed and sputtered into her handkerchief.

The girls had never seen Nan-Nan with a handkerchief. Mum said they were just big bacterial gro-bags.

Catty's whole demeanour changed. They thought she'd recoil in disgust, but instead she approached Nan-Nan and smiled like the Joker, showing her teeth. 'Oh, you poor dear,' she said, leaning over her. 'I'm so glad you found us.'

'My grandsons were saying there might be nicer hotels,' said Nan-Nan. 'But Catty's Cattery, well, it's special, isn't it?'

'So special,' agreed Catty, soothingly.

'And it's got such character,' added Nan-Nan.

'Think she means *characters*,' said Ali, under her breath. 'Who knew that Nan-Nan was this good an actress? That sounds nothing like her.'

'Yeah, I'm regretting not picking an accent,' said Tulip. 'Would have been fun if we got to do accents! I love drama at school.' Ali looked at her scornfully, because this was true. Tulip was always getting picked for the good parts with the most lines. Ali only ever got to be Gangster Number 4, which mainly involved pushing people around.

'And is this shy darling one of your grandsons?' said Catty, looking simperingly at Jay.

Jay nodded and shook his head, indecisive with panic.

'They're not big talkers,' said Nan-Nan

hastily. 'Their English isn't that great. They've just come from a very violent regime.'

Jay rolled his eyes.

'Have I met you before?' asked Catty, 'You seem so . . . familiar.'

'In another life, perhaps?' said Nan-Nan. 'I'm VERY spiritual. Or perhaps on the internet. I went on a lot of dating sites, when I lost my darling wife. Are you single?'

'Your wife? Single?' sputtered Catty. 'Oh, I see, um no, I'm not on the dating sites.' Then she asked curiously, 'Are they any good?'

'Well, here I am, dying alone,' shrugged Nan-Nan. 'You tell me.'

Hidden behind the door, Ali and Tulip were stuffing their hands over their mouths to keep themselves from laughing out loud. Zac was looking worried about Jay being out in the splash zone.

'It always started off well,' carried on Nan-Nan, 'until my dates realized I was just a penniless old fool.'

'Oh? Penniless?' said Catty. Her demeanour changed again. She became business-like and dismissive. 'Right then, nice to meet you and your grandson. Enjoy your stay. Talk to Manny if you need anything.'

'Yes, *penniless*,' said Nan-Nan. 'I don't have pennies. I have boats, cars and houses. But not,' she scoffed slightly, saying the word dismissively, with distaste, 'pennies.'

Catty's eyes widened like saucers and her painted eyebrows hit the roof. 'What did you say?'

'Well, aristocrats don't carry loose change,' said Nan-Nan, slyly. 'You know, you look familiar too?'

'Oh,' said Catty, taking Nan-Nan's arm. 'Maybe that's because I'm very spiritual too. I think we were definitely BEST FRIENDS in a former life. Now do come for tea . . .'

'Go and play,' said Nan-Nan meaningfully to Jay.

'Um yeah, OK,' said Jay.

The girls and Zac came out into the corridor when the coast was Catty-clear.

'So, what was that about?' said Jay. 'It's quite obvious that revolting woman is only interested in your Nan-Nan for her cash. Her intentions are clearly dishonourable.'

'It was about pumping Catty for information,' said Ali. 'Duh.'

'Do you think Catty is preying on all these old dudes?' said Tulip. 'Sounds like she's the one getting them to leave their money to this place if they kick the bucket?'

'More like *when* they kick the bucket,' said Zac, sadly. 'Your nan's the healthiest person here.'

'There was something really familiar about that woman,' mused Jay. 'Didn't like her at all. She gave me the creeps.'

'I said that the moment I saw her,' said Zac.

'I thought so too,' said Tulip, 'She has this really chilling vibe. Like . . . I don't know, Cruella de Ville or Monty Burns or someone.'

'Who are they?' asked Zac. 'Political dictators?'

Ali looked like she was about to scoff, but Tulip nudged her. It wasn't the boys' fault they weren't allowed to watch much telly. The first time they'd seen a 12-rated film was over at Ali and Tulip's house a few weeks ago.

'They're criminal characters. Basically the sort of baddie to make coats and slippers outta small cute furry animals,' she explained. 'Or pollute the planet.'

Jay looked horrified. 'That's awful! Did they

get caught?'

'Um, yeah,' said Tulip. 'Let's go with that.' She was distracted by Ali shaking the handle of the door to Catty's room.

'Whadya doing?' she asked, as Ali stuck her foot against the door and yanked harder at the handle.

'Breaking in, duh,' she said. 'Give me a hand.'

'Um, I would, but,' started Zac, hesitantly.

'But what?' snapped Ali. 'Against your morals, is it? Get over yourself, goody-goody!'

'It's more that you're pulling it more shut,' said Jay. 'It's a push, not a pull.' And he gently gave the handle a jiggle and turn, and pushed it open.

Ali looked at him scornfully. 'You're trying so hard not to smirk right now, aren't you?'

'So hard,' said Jay. Then he burst into a grin. 'Nope, not trying at all. Come on.'

'Good powers of observation,' said Tulip, following him in with Ali. 'They must come with the specs.'

Zac hung back, looking worried. Ali had been right, he really didn't like breaking and entering.

'It's fine,' Tulip said, patting him on the shoulder. 'You can be the lookout guy.'

Zac grinned too, gratefully. 'That's my jam.'
He sat on the floor outside, guarding the door.

'Wow,' said Ali, stepping into the room.

'Wow,' said Tulip, standing beside her.

'Wowsers,' said Jay, just to be different. Ali
rolled her eyes at him.

It was like the door had swung open into a
different building altogether. Like a posh hotel
from one of Mum's period dramas.

Instead of the plastic lino that was in their
room, there were wall-to-wall rugs that were
so thick that their feet sank into them. There
was wallpaper with gold floral designs, instead
of the beige and cream wipe-clean gloss. An
enormous four poster bed covered in fat, smug-
looking cushions in gold and green. Dark,
glossy furniture with carved details and ornate
metal handles nestled in the corners of the
room. A chandelier twinkled with glass droplets
in the weak sunlight which filtered through the
windows.

A strange oldie-worldly contraption sat on a
leather-topped desk. It was made of shiny black
metal, with numbers printed around the edge of
a spinning circle, and there was a detachable bit
that sat hooked on top of the machine. It didn't

seem to be doing anything, but it was plugged into the wall.

'Nice to know where the budget for Catty's Cattery is going,' said Tulip in disgust. 'Those poor old folks are eating stuff labelled So-Sausagey in plastic packets, and Catty's living in luxury.'

'Her clock's weird,' said Ali, pointing to the shiny black contraption. 'It starts at zero and only goes up to nine. And what's the handle thing on top for?'

'That's not a clock,' said Jay. 'It's a home phone.'

'What's a home phone?' asked Tulip. She looked at Ali, who shrugged.

'Well, what's the tough bit?' said Jay. 'Home or phone?'

'You're a bit of a jerk, sometimes,' said Ali. 'And I'm saying "a bit" to be polite.'

'Oh, sorry,' said Jay, 'I thought you were joking. It's just like a communal phone that sits plugged in at home.'

'What's the point of that?' asked Tulip, frowning. 'It would only work if someone was near it. Why wouldn't you call their mobile, instead?'

'It's from before mobiles,' said Jay. 'Like when there were butlers always hanging about who could take messages for their bosses.'

'Guessing it's the butler's day off,' said Ali, looking around the grand room, and sitting on the four-poster bed. She gave it an experimental bounce. 'Half expecting to see one wander in with a tray of tea and scones.'

'Home phone,' said Tulip. 'Huh.' She looked around the machine, curiously. 'How does it work?'

'I'll show you,' said Jay. 'Dad keeps old stuff like this in the shed.' He picked up the handle, and spun his finger around the circle, and dialled his own number.

When he'd finished, they heard Jay's phone beep plaintively.

'Even your ring tone is whiny,' said Ali, unwilling to admit that she was impressed he'd managed to work the thing.

Tulip had started looking through the bureau. 'Papers, papers, papers,' she said. 'And a massive box of these,' she held out a print-out of a form, which said, 'Last Will and Testament.'

She pulled out a leather briefcase, stashed beside the desk, and starting unbuckling it.

'Probably more papers,' Ali said. 'Bit of a pain. Thought there'd be an iPad or something. Then we could've just scrolled through her messages.'

'Oh,' Tulip said, peering into the briefcase, once she had finally got it open. 'That's surprising.' It was full of medical kit, with boxes and bottles of pills, and needles for injections. 'Suppose someone has to have medical training in a nursing home.'

Just then, a tinny ringing filled the air. The old-fashioned phone was rattling on the desk.

They all froze.

'Stop it ringing,' hissed Ali. 'Catty'll come back if she hears that.'

'I don't know how to stop it ringing!' whispered Tulip, who was closest. 'Maybe it'll go to voicemail.'

'It can't have voicemail!' said Jay. 'It's pre-voicemail! It's like expecting a gramophone to have voicemail!'

'A what?' said Ali.

'You know,' said Jay, 'a record player?'

'A what?' said Tulip.

Jay rolled his eyes. 'You two know *nothing* about old stuff! The only way you stop it ringing is by taking the receiver off the hook!' And he picked it up to demonstrate.

And then his eyes widened, as they all realized what he'd done.

He'd answered the phone.

'Hello!' said a voice down the line. 'Mumsy?'

'Say something!' hissed Ali.

'Don't say anything!' whispered Tulip.

'Mumsy!' said Manny, insistently. 'You there? Are you alright?'

Jay panicked and answered in a fake female voice that didn't sound much like Catty at all.

'New phone, who dis?' he said, clearly hoping that Manny would think he'd rung a wrong number.

'Hahaha,' said Manny. 'It's just me, Mumsy. Was calling to let you know that I've got the bank details of the . . .' He trailed off.

'Mm-hmm?' mumbled Jay, uncertainly.

'Sorry, Mumsy,' said Manny. 'I thought I called you on the land line, but I swear I just saw you walking around the lounge with the new guest.'

'Oh,' quavered Jay. 'Mobile?'

'Yup, must've called your mobile. I'll just come and find you,' said Manny. They heard him calling out, 'Ahoy, Mumsy!' just before the call clicked off.

Jay hung up the receiver. 'Um, so that's how you stop it ringing,' he said sheepishly. 'You unhook it, and then hang it up.'

'And now Manny's telling Catty that he's just been on the phone to her,' said Tulip, rapidly closing up the briefcase.

Jay's phone started ringing again. 'Did you just hit redial?' asked Ali in annoyance.

'I keep telling you that old phones don't do stuff like that,' said Jay, looking at his phone. 'It's my bro.' He answered it, putting it on speakerphone. 'What's up, Zac-Zac?'

'Watch out, she's coming back,' said Zac. 'And she's looking cross. At least, I think she is. It's hard to tell under all the stuff plastered on her face.'

They froze, as they heard thumping footsteps, and then heard Catty snapping at Zac. 'What are you doing, loitering there?'

'Oh mighty beans and chickpeas,' Zac whispered, and then said too loudly, '*Hide*-and-seek. HIDE-and-seek. I'm counting. Ninety-eight, ninety-nine, one hundred! Ready or not, here I come!'

The others looked at each other.

'You heard what he said,' Tulip waved a hand around the room, 'HIDE!'

The door handle was turning. The girls slid under the grand four-poster and Jay dashed behind a pair of heavy brocade curtains.

The girls saw Catty's big shiny shoes walk into the room and up to the desk. They heard her dialling the disc on the old phone.

'Ahoy,' she called out, into the phone. And then she said, 'Manny, I think I'm going to have to review your medication. You're hallucinating . . .'

'But Mumsy,' they heard Manny pleading over the phone, 'you were definitely there. I mean you're there now. Aren't you?' He suddenly sounded unsure. 'What if you're not really there? And you're not you? I'm feeling all confused again, Mumsy. What if I'm not really ME?'

'Get back to work, Manny,' snapped Catty. 'Get our new guest a seat in the lounge. Make it a comfortable one that she can't get out of easily. I'm bringing ALL the paperwork.'

She collected the briefcase and a stack of papers, and stomped back out of the room.

The girls turned to each other, sliding out

from under the bed. 'You know what, she's got massive feet,' said Tulip.

'Yeah, and she wobbled a lot on the flat heels she was wearing earlier, for someone who likes striding around so much,' added Ali.

'She's got tartan slippers hidden here behind the curtain,' piped up Jay, unrolling himself awkwardly from the heavy brocade.

'Why would you hide slippers?' said Tulip.

'Maybe she nicked them from someone,' said Jay. 'They've got someone else's initials, monogrammed with gold thread.'

'Of course they have,' said Ali. 'This whole room feels like it's been nicked from a film set.'

'Or other people's houses,' said Tulip. 'Maybe Catty isn't just liberating them of their cash, but all their stuff.'

Tulip yanked open the wardrobe door. There were men's suits lined up neatly, as well as new women's clothes, still with their labels.

'Do you think Manny shares the room with his mum?' asked Ali. 'A bit icky, right?'

'Maybe he's just using the wardrobe space,' suggested Jay. 'Though he doesn't seem the type to wear posh suits.'

'I'm thinking he's not the only one using the

wardrobe space,' said Tulip, and she pulled out a trench coat. 'Isn't this Nan-Nan's? How did Catty get it?'

'It's not Nan-Nan's. Catty was wearing a trench coat before, in the garden.' Ali frowned. 'Didn't think anything of it.'

Something didn't add up. But before she could work it out, Zac came running into the room. 'Guys, I think we should go help your nan, that Catty is going after her like she's her supper tonight. And your nan's so committed, I don't know how she's gonna get out of it.'

'*Let's go!*' said Ali. 'Before Nan-Nan signs all her worldly goods to the Cattery.'

'You've met your nan,' said Jay. 'She wouldn't do that.'

'Normally she wouldn't,' said Tulip. 'But I'm a bit worried that we've found out how Catty is quite so persuasive with the pensioners.' She pulled a little vial of medication and a needle from the trench coat.

'Enough for you, nerd? Let's go!' said Ali to Jay, running out. 'I hate that you made me repeat myself!'

CHAPTER 17:
CATTY SHOWS HER CLAWS

They raced down the dingy corridors, and saw Nan-Nan, leaning on her cane, refusing to take the deep and squashy seat that Manny kept offering her.

'Do take a seat, your ladyship,' Manny was pleading. 'Please.' It was like he knew he'd get in trouble if she didn't.

'No need, dear,' said Nan-Nan. 'I keep telling you that I'm fine.'

'But you'll be so much more comfortable,' cooed Manny. 'Mumsy says she's got a lot of paperwork to discuss with you.'

'Nothing very arduous,' said Catty. 'Just the usual conditions of a Catty's Cattery stay.' She was leaning relentlessly towards Nan-Nan, with the briefcase and a sheaf of papers in her hand.

She smiled that Joker smile. Too many teeth.

The briefcase full of meds and needles. The meds and needles in the pockets.

Something in Tulip's head niggled. Alarmingly.

'After all, we're just one big happy family, here,' said Catty.

'Happy families,' nodded Manny, with a big, cheesy smile, putting an arm around Catty. She swatted him off, impatiently. 'Sorry, Mumsy.'

Happy families. Cheesy smile.

Something in Ali's head niggled.

Nan-Nan was looking between Manny, the bearded double of Evelyn-Sprotland, and Catty, towering over her in her flat shoes.

And then Nan-Nan's eyes flashed. It was like something in her head had lit up like a Christmas tree.

'Nan-Nan knows something!' whispered Ali, triumphantly.

'What does she know?' whispered Zac. He looked in confusion at the others, but they just looked blank.

'Well, thank you, my dears,' said Nan-Nan, dropping her little-old-lady act. 'You've given me just what I need. I must say, this has been a VERY informative stay.'

'Your voice just changed,' said Catty, frowning with confusion.

'So did your face, dear,' said Nan-Nan. 'Seeing as you've got two of them, I shouldn't be surprised.' She turned to go. 'Well, I have no intention of extending *my* stay to the end of my days, as your charming cat poster has urged. I think I'd better collect my grandkids and go.'

'Oh no, don't go,' said Manny. 'I hope we haven't upset you.' He seemed genuinely sorry.

'But I'll keep these papers, if I may,' and Nan-Nan began striding off, decisively. She wasn't faking her limp any more, either.

'Oh no,' hissed Catty. 'I'm afraid, your ladyship, that those papers are confidential, and if you're not staying . . .'

She tried to tug the papers out of Nan-Nan's hands, and Nan-Nan tugged back, hard. And then Catty stumbled, falling into Nan-Nan and knocking her over.

'Nan-Nan,' shrieked Tulip and Ali, and they raced over, rolling a spare wheelchair into place just in time, so that Nan-Nan fell neatly into the chair, with Catty sprawled on top of her.

'Mumsy!' shrieked Manny, and he pulled Catty off Nan-Nan.

Catty's over-sized cats-eye shades had come off, and Nan-Nan's hair had fallen out of her scarf, in flowing silver and black waves.

Catty stared at Nan-Nan, sitting in the wheelchair, like she'd seen a ghost. 'You!' she said, 'You, You, You . . .'

'I think she's having a stroke,' said Tulip. 'Her face is definitely sagging, though that might be the make-up sliding off.'

'And you!' whispered Catty, turning her head at Tulip's voice. Tulip patted her head, and realized that her cap and wig had fallen off when she'd dived under Catty's bed. 'And you!' Now she was staring at Ali, who was looking defiantly back at her. 'You called her Nan-Nan . . .'

'Can you raise your arms?' asked Tulip, checking for symptoms. 'Can you smile and show me your teeth?'

Ali whacked her. 'She's not having a stroke, noob.' Catty looked more like she was about to explode.

'We've been *made*, girls,' said Nan-Nan.

'Job's done! Let's get outta here,' and she began wheeling the chair expertly out of the room, with impressive speed. The twins raced after her.

'Get-that-guest!' screamed Catty. 'She's a *mole*!'

'No, no, Mumsy,' said Manny soothingly. 'She's got a *cat*, not a mole. But I'm not sure where it is. Last saw it hunting rats.'

Witch chose that moment to make an appearance. She leapt furiously on Catty, snarling and clawing at her clothes.

'Noooo, geroff,' shouted Catty, in a surprisingly deep voice. She flung Witchy away with equal fury and, kicking off her smart flats, went chasing after Nan-Nan, with Manny chasing after her.

'Mumsy,' said Manny, 'it's fine! We can let a guest go. It's just a residence. Not a prison.'

Catty turned on him. 'You know NOTHING, you stupid, useless little man. You've ALWAYS known nothing! Now go get me that granny!'

Nan-Nan didn't have all-terrain wheels, but they headed straight for the woods, where Catty couldn't spot them, and disappeared into the trees. They were almost at her car, on the dirt track in the woods where Nan-Nan had parked up earlier that day with the boys, when Tulip realized that Jay and Zac weren't running with them.

'What about the boys?' said Tulip breathlessly, as she reached the Nan-mobile.

'Too late for them,' said Ali. 'Snoozers, losers.'

'I've messaged them to meet us here in the woods,' said Nan-Nan crossly to Ali. 'We don't leave people behind.'

'Um, yeah, we're already here,' said Zac, waving sheepishly from the back seat.

'Yeah, thanks for that kick in the face,' said Jay to Ali. 'You're really not a team player. I'm surprised Tulip made it out of the womb in one piece.'

'Great work, boys,' said Tulip, relieved to see them. 'How'd you get here so fast?'

'We asked the gardener-security guys to give us a lift, they were heading this way to dig holes or something,' said Zac. 'They used an old golf cart.'

'You mean, you *told* them where we were going?' said Nan-Nan, in disbelief. 'You showed them exactly where we were!'

A Cattery-branded car screeched up the dirt

track and U-turned in front of them, blocking Nan-Nan and the girls from Jay and Zac.

And Manny and Catty got out. Catty was wielding a syringe, and she walked up to the Nan-mobile, smiling maliciously.

'Your ladyship,' she said, with sickening smugness, gesturing to Nan-Nan's car. 'Your chariot awaits.'

'You always liked your drama, didn't you?' said Nan-Nan. 'Well, we've got you now.'

The girls exchanged a quick look. 'Nan-Nan KNOWS her!' whispered Tulip, in shock.

'No,' said Catty, 'you've profoundly misread the situation. *We've* got *you*.' She gestured to the boys. 'I'm taking SOMEONE away with me in your car. You can choose who it is. I don't care.'

'Oh, fine,' shrugged Nan-Nan, and she rolled over to her Nan-Mobile. 'Get out, boys.'

'Nan-Nan, NO!' said Tulip.

'Don't sacrifice yourself for them!' said Ali. 'No offence, boys.'

'Some taken,' said Zac.

'Seriously, Tulip, how were you not EATEN in the womb by her?' muttered Jay.

'That's a teensy bit hurtful,' huffed Ali. She

ran forward to stop Nan-Nan, but was pulled back by Tulip.

'Nan-Nan knows what she's doing,' whispered Tulip. And she added to Jay, 'And you shouldn't joke about the twin-eating thing in the womb. That sort of happens. Twin-to-twin transfusion. One bro or sister sucks all the life out of the other one. Nicks all their nutrients. It's really sad.'

'What?' said Manny. He looked like he'd been struck in the face. 'One bro sucks the life out of the other?'

'Shut up, Manny,' said Catty in a different, deeper voice. 'Get educated in your own time. Read the runt's stupid blog.'

'How'd you know I have a blog?' said Tulip. 'I've got like four followers.'

Nan-Nan went to get in the car, but Catty opened the boot instead.

'You must think I'm stupid, if you think I'm going to let you sit behind me with those lethal weapons screwed onto your knees,' she said. 'I'm the smart one! Manny's the stupid one.'

'Mumsy!' said Manny. 'Now that's a bit hurtful.'

'Oh give up the act,' snapped Nan-Nan. 'And

we all know his name isn't Manny. I mean Manny Gers the manager? When they were handing out imagination you must've been hitting up the stupid tree instead.'

'My name isn't Manny?' said Manny, looking confused. 'What does she mean, Mumsy?'

'The poor guy. He really doesn't know?' said Nan-Nan. 'What shall I tell him?'

Catty laughed cruelly. She said, 'You know what I like about you, Ruby? It's that you put the children first.'

Ali stiffened. 'She KNOWS Nan-Nan,' she hissed to Tulip. 'She even knows her name!'

Nan-Nan stiffened too. 'Leave Minnie and the girls out of this.'

Catty shrugged. 'That's up to you.' She waved the syringe.

'Oh for goodness sake, you and your tedious amateur dramatics,' said Nan-Nan, and she swung herself into the boot of the car. 'Ugh, you left the street trash from back home in here,' she complained to the girls. 'It stinks.'

'Nooo!' said Tulip. 'Who is she? Who are *they*? Tell us, Nan-Nan!'

'You KNOW her!' said Ali. 'You must do! Tell us, now, before she carts you off.'

'Hah!' said Catty. 'Tell them! I dare you!
And say goodbye to the kids, FOREVER.'

'Is Manny really Sprotland?' asked Ali,
desperately.

'I still don't know what that means,'
complained Manny. 'Mumsy, what's happening?'

'Oh dear, girls,' said Catty. 'You'll have to
do better than that. Evelyn Sprotland is dead,
remember? You buried him. And he's never
coming back.'

She pushed a weakly protesting Manny into the
car. Then she jumped in herself, still shoe-less,
and she drove off, giving them the finger.

'Oh, mighty beans and chickpeas,' said Zac.
'I think your nan's just been kidnapped.'

Ali turned on him fiercely. 'WHERE is that
golf cart?'

CHAPTER 18:
TWO IN THE HOLE

'What?' said Zac. 'You want the golf cart?' He was looking helplessly at Nan-Nan's car, as she was being driven off. Tears were running down his face.

'We should call the police!' said Jay.

'Yeah, *you* call the police,' said Tulip. 'You're the backroom kids. We're going after Nan-Nan.'

'You can't go after your nan,' said Zac. 'You haven't got a responsible adult with you. It's not like you can call Momo to come over and be your designated driver.'

'Look, you big bug,' said Ali, 'it might have

escaped your notice, but all our responsible adults have been stabbed, or are stuck in the hospital.'

'Yeah,' said Jay, 'it's like someone's got a vendetta against you guys.'

'Maybe it's safer here without Catty and Manny, anyway,' said Zac. 'They're a disgrace to the hotel business. I'm deffo gonna call the police. And then child support services, 'cause we're four vulnerable children.'

'Argh!' said Ali. 'It's not all about you! Our Nan-Nan's been nan-napped and you're worried about whether we've got appropriate adult supervision!'

'Tulip?' Zac pleaded with her, as the more sensible one. She shook her head violently, and grabbed Ali's hand, and started running back through the woods with her.

'Ali's right,' she yelled over her shoulder. 'It's not about us. It's about Nan-Nan!'

Tulip and Ali raced back towards the hotel, and Ali didn't even try to shake off Tulip's hand. If anything, she squeezed it tighter. Tulip looked at her, questioningly.

'Shut up,' said Ali. But then she squeezed Tulip's hand again. 'You had my back. You actually said I was right.'

'You can be mean and right at the same time,' said Tulip.

They found the golf cart, parked up on the long drive that led to Catty's Cattery. They jumped in. The flaw in their plan suddenly seemed a bit obvious.

'You know how to drive this thing?' Tulip asked Ali.

'That's what YouTube is for,' said Ali, staring at her phone while fiddling with levers and buttons. The golf cart started, and jerked backwards. And then Ali managed to get it going forward. 'So that's forward, and that's the brakes,' she said. 'Just like a dodgem. Let's go.'

She was heading back up the road, jerkily, when she asked, 'Um, d'you know which way? Once we get to the main road?'

'I guess that's what Google Maps is for,' said Tulip. 'They could be taking Nan-Nan anywhere. But we might catch them if they stop, there's only one road that leads to the motorway.'

Far ahead, they caught sight of Greasy and Frankenstein, who had dropped Zac and Jay in the woods.

'Ugh, them,' said Ali, hitting the accelerator.

'Stop!' shrieked Tulip. 'You can't run them over. That's not nice at all.'

'You've got a serious problem about needing to be liked,' scoffed Ali. 'Think you've been hanging out with Zac too much.'

'Hey, you!' yelled the groundskeepers. 'That's our golf cart!'

'Yeah, we're bringing it back to you,' called Tulip, helpfully.

'Yep, that's exactly what we're doing!' said Ali, and she slammed the pedal to the metal. 'On our way!'

'You gotta brake, idiot kids!' yelled the bigger guy. The cart was swaying dangerously from side to side.

'Trying-to-work-out-which-one's-the-brake!' Ali yelled, not too convincingly.

The groundskeepers were running desperately away from the golf cart, terrified she was going to run into them.

'Stop! You maniac kids!'

'They're insane!' yelled the other guy. 'Crazy-creepy twins!'

'What are you doing?' asked Tulip, holding on hard to stop herself falling out of the cart.

'The road's that way.'

'Catch up!' said Ali. 'You know this bit of the woods. We really FELL for it before.'

Tulip grinned, as she got it. And just then, the men both screamed 'AAARGH' and fell into a hole. The same one that they had trapped Tulip in before.

Ali floored the other pedal, and brought the golf cart to a crashing halt, just before the hole. It trembled on the edge for a moment, and then rocked and rolled. Before stopping completely.

'Hey, I found the brake,' called Ali to the goons. 'No thanks to you guys, you were rubbish.'

Tulip climbed out, and saw them sitting crumpled and furious at the bottom of the pit.

'Everyone all right?' she said, with a sweet smile. 'Show me four thumbs!' And she did a double-thumbs up.

'Get us OUT OF HERE!' Greasy roared at her.

'Are you sure?' winced Frankenstein, rubbing his bruised behind. 'I think the safest place is wherever those two aren't! Maybe we should just stay down here until they go.'

'Oh, that's disappointing,' said Ali, climbing

down from the golf cart, and peering into the hole with Tulip. 'I thought they'd be face down in the pit. Not sitting up.'

She yelled down to them. 'You're really not committing to the whole pit-bit, are you?'

The bigger guy shuddered, and said to his colleague, 'She's insane! She thinks we're pit people!'

'I think at some level, you always knew this would happen,' said Tulip, kindly.

They were surprised by Zac and Jay running through the woods, and joining them, breathlessly. Zac pulled out his blue inhaler and sucked down noisily on it.

'Oh,' he said. 'Hole-diving? That looks fun.'

'Let's go,' said Jay. 'While you've been pushing people into holes for funsies, we've been doing the unsung-hero backroom stuff.'

'What, you called child support services?' said Ali, sarcastically.

'Better than that,' said Zac. 'Got us a ride.'

They heard a honking horn, and LeRoi calling out, 'Hurry up! My laxatives are kicking in, so I've only got thirty minutes to get to the service station.'

'Aww, you're amazing!' said Tulip, putting her arms around Jay and Zac.

'Yeah, about time you guys pulled your weight,' sniffed Ali, and squealed with protest as Zac pulled her into the hug.

'Lemme go, lame-os,' she complained, extracting herself with Jay's help.

'So lame,' agreed Jay. 'Zac's always rugby-tackling me with hugs at home.'

'Hugby tackling!' corrected Zac, jumping back on Jay with his arms around his neck.

'Someone from the house will come and get you,' said Tulip to the groundskeeper goons. 'We'll call them when we're on our way. Sorry, but nobody stops us from saving our Nan-Nan.'

'Now there's four of them!' whimpered the bigger goon, pointing a trembling finger. 'It's like an alien invasion.'

'Twin-vasion!' said Tulip, fist-bumping Ali and pulling back with wavy fingers. 'I like that! I'll use that for my blog.'

'Do you guys need anything?' asked Zac helpfully, looking in the golf cart. 'There's cans of prunes for a snack, and some toilet roll. That should cover the basics, for a while.' He tossed them down to the men.

Tulip beamed at him for his concern. Jay shrugged, but looked a bit cross, as though Zac had shown him up.

And Ali, she just shuddered.

'Prunes?' she said, shaking her head. 'Oh no, Zac. That's another level of cruel. And you guys say that I'M the mean one.'

CHAPTER 19:
DRAMA LLAMA, KARMA LLAMA

LeRoi was singing his random Elvis songs all the way to the service station, as they crawled down the motorway slow lane. At least the kids thought they were Elvis songs, he was wobbling his head a lot and finished each one with 'Uh-thank-you-very-much' in his dodgy American accent.

'Could you speed up, grandpa?' complained Ali.

'Not without my haemorrhoid doughnut cushion,' said LeRoi. 'Putting the foot on the gas makes my bottom uncomfortable.'

'Ugh, TMI,' said Ali.

'You're welcome,' said LeRoi, grinning broadly. 'Thanks for getting me out on the road again. Haven't driven for years.'

'Um, you do have a license, right?' asked Zac.

'Definitely. Well I mean, I definitely *had* one,' LeRoi corrected himself. 'Passed on my ninth attempt. Kept meaning to get it renewed, ten years ago, but stuff came up. You know, with the civil revolution and the hurricane evacuation and winning the National Championships and then I got into an argument with my bestie and got kicked out of our water aerobics class, which was just the WORST . . .'

Zac and Jay and Tulip all opened their mouths to speak, but Ali frowned them all down.

'NO follow-up questions!' she said. 'Don't ask him a thing about his surprisingly fascinating life journey. We'll be here all day.' She looked crossly at Jay.

'Nice work, noob,' she muttered to him. 'You got us a driver without a license who probably got passed through pity.'

'More luck than pity,' said LeRoi. 'The roads were empty, there was a curfew or something, because of the bombings, or the snipers, or both. I passed my test during the war. Forget which one.'

'That checks out,' said Tulip. 'Our Nan-Nan says stuff like that a lot.'

Where's LeRoi gonna take us?' asked Jay. 'We don't even know where they've taken your nan.'

Tulip was staring at her phone.

'OMG, Insta-geek,' said Ali, knocking it out of her hand. 'Were you really checking your BLOG? Not the time to update it with your TWINspirational messages.'

'Catty said she saw the blog,' protested Tulip. 'Was just checking if she'd left any messages there. And I like twinspirational, so I'm keeping that. I'm gonna put it on this cat poster series I've just designed. Witch is the star.'

'Like the fat cat needs more attention,' complained Ali.

'I need the loo,' said LeRoi cheerfully. 'Desperately. Pulling in here.'

Ali had started staring at her phone, too.

'Hey, back at ya, Insta-geek,' said Tulip.

'Shush,' said Ali, 'I'm thinking. How did Nan-Nan KNOW Catty?' She put her phone away in frustration. 'She's not texted us anything.'

'She must be terrified in the boot of that car,'

said Zac.

'If Catty and Manny knew Nan-Nan, they'd be terrified that she's IN the boot of the car,' said Tulip defiantly, fist-bumping with Ali.

'Yeah, she works one of these wigs,' said Tulip, pulling Ali's off her head. 'And a trench coat, and she's basically a super nan.'

'And she's got a whole super nan-witch-clan,' agreed Ali. 'OMG, we've gotta get in touch with the SWAT team. They can trench-coat-up and save her!'

'Trench coat?' repeated Jay. 'Catty has one, too. And she had a load of wigs. I saw them stuffed in a bag behind the curtain, when I was hiding there.'

'A trench coat is basically schooliform for adults. Like jeans,' pointed out Ali.

'Even I've got an old trench coat somewhere,' LeRoi agreed. 'Really suited me.' He parked the car, and got out painfully slowly. 'Oh, I've got stiff since I stopped doing the water aerobics,' he complained. He strolled off to the loo. 'I may be some time.'

They all got out of the car while they were waiting for LeRoi.

'So we know that Catty knew Nan-Nan, as she called her Ruby. And Nan-Nan knew Catty, too,' said Tulip slowly, like she was piecing it together.

'They deffo had history,' agreed Zac. 'And not a nice history. Didn't seem that they were school buddies.'

'And Catty had a trench coat and wigs, that she hid,' said Ali, less slowly.

'I guess lots of baldy old biddies wear wigs,' said Tulip, doubtfully. 'What were they like, Jay?'

'Dunno,' said Jay, 'there were loads of them. Different colours. Curly.'

'Curly!' Tulip yelped.

Ali grinned, and slapped Jay on the forehead.

'Ouch!' said Jay. 'You slap yourself on the forehead. Not me!'

'Just trying to keep you involved,' said Ali. 'We've just worked out that . . .'

'Catty was on the SWAT team!' Tulip and Ali said together. 'Jinx!' they said, annoyed. 'Jinx, padlock, 1-2-3!'

'Ooh. She's ex-SWAT team, you mean? But she's gone ROGUE!' said Zac. 'So she's a ROGUE ex Senior Water Aerobics Training team operative. That's why your nan knows her. And that's why they hate each other.'

Ali and Tulip looked at him, so furious that they couldn't speak.

'Oh, is it cool that I said all that?' added Zac. 'I didn't steal your big finish, did I?'

Tulip shook her head, but Ali nodded, ferociously. So ferociously that she'd have headbutted him if he hadn't jumped back.

'So,' said Zac, preparing to break the jinx before Ali broke something, 'Tul . . .'

But Jay put his hand over his mouth. 'Don't!' he said warningly. 'Seriously, let's enjoy the silence.' He grinned, and sat on the bonnet, lying back and stretching his long legs.

Ali texted furiously, 'BREAK THE JINX, JERKFACE,' and showed it to him on her screen.

'Hah,' said Jay. 'Yeah, deffo gonna do that, seeing as you ask so politely.' He closed his eyes and hummed.

Ali shook him and showed him the screen again, 'BREAK THE JINX, JERKFACE, PLEASE.'

'See, not so hard,' said Jay. 'Still not tempted. Say something *nice.*'

'YOUR CLOTHES ARE REALLY COOL,' wrote Ali.

'Thanks,' said Jay, before realizing something. 'Oh wait, these are YOUR clothes. You're just taking credit for your own stuff.'

Ali looked smug.

Tulip sighed, and wrote on her phone, 'IF CATTY'S ROGUE SWAT, WE SHOULDN'T GET IN TOUCH WITH THEM. SHE MIGHT'VE TURNED SOMEONE ELSE ON THE TEAM.'

'Oh honestly,' said Zac, taking her screen to squint at it, breaking the jinx himself. 'Tulip, Ali, impressed by the speed-texting, but let's just think about this. Your nan's team must have some intel on Catty?'

'You'd think,' said Ali, 'but they just sent us to case out the Cattery with Nan-Nan because of some dodgy cash donations. I don't think they knew much about it at all. That's what *we* were there for.'

'But Catty could be in league with Silver, or any of the others,' argued Tulip. 'Or she could be impersonating them, if she's got all the wigs in different colours. Framing them, even. Can I have my phone back, please?'

'Sure,' said Zac, handing it back to her. 'Cool llama app, how does that work?'

'Dunno,' said Tulip. 'It's something Ali put on my phone a while back. It's like a friending app for virtual llamas. But it's soooo cute. Look, Drama Llama is best friends with Karma Llama. They're always together.'

'Excuse me,' said Ali, 'I didn't put that lame llama app on your phone. You put it on mine.'

'Nope, nah-ha,' said Tulip. 'You put it on mine. Look, I've got the message you sent, "Lame llamas for you, lame-o, I know how you luuurve dumb fluffy things haha 'coz you are one, LOL" and then you put a laughing-crying-emoji and a llama and a heart.'

'Sounds just like me,' admitted Ali. 'But I didn't write it. And look, I've got the message YOU sent, "OMG I LOVE LLAMAS. Don't be a drama-llama be a karma-llama!" and then you sent me a link to some video of cute baby llamas on YouTube so I just ignored it.'

'Sounds like me, too,' admitted Tulip. She frowned, and began pacing thoughtfully up and down. 'But it definitely wasn't.'

'Someone's hacked your phones, then?' said Zac.

'And someone who knows you pretty well, AND has access to your phones,' said Jay. He jumped back and scrambled off the bonnet of the car, as Ali leapt for him with her nails out like claws.

'Hey, I didn't mean ME!' he said, pushing her off. 'I don't know you well enough to imitate your text-speak, and I definitely couldn't make up lame llama rhymes.'

'Not me either,' said Zac, hurrying around the car after his brother. 'I'd have gone for hedgehogs, or alpacas, or vegan foods, or something.'

'And Mum and Dad limit our online access and screen time,' added Jay, as Ali was now chasing them around the car. 'I wouldn't know about llama apps! I mean what does it even do?'

Tulip stopped pacing. She held up her phone triumphantly. 'It's gotta be a location app,' she said. She was grinning, insanely.

'What are you so happy about?' said Ali. 'Someone's hacked our phones!'

'Tell me,' said Tulip, 'the only person we know who's techy enough to hack our phones, knows our text-speak, AND has access to them.'

'Nan-Nan,' breathed Ali. She looked around,

expectantly, but there was nothing. 'Sorry, for a moment I thought she'd roll out from behind the cars with a slow handclap.'

Tulip sat on the kerb, and patted the place beside her in a business-like manner. 'We always wondered how Nan-Nan knew where we were. Like that time we ran away and she found us resuscitating someone on the underground.'

'I thought she'd hidden tracking on our phones, but couldn't find anything,' said Ali, joining her. 'She didn't hide it. She left it in plain sight. On a llama app!'

'She's good,' nodded Tulip. 'Look, you and I must be Drama Llama and Karma Llama, that's why they were always together whenever I looked at it.' She clicked on the cute characters, and some random numbers came up.

'Well, that's a bit dumb, it's not saying where we are,' said Ali.

'Yep, it is,' said Zac, typing the numbers into his own phone. 'They're coordinates. For this service station.'

'The location app works! So who's Lovely Llama?' asked Jay, looking at the llamas roaming around their virtual town on the screen. 'Guessed straight away it isn't you.'

'Haha,' said Ali. 'Deffo not you, either.' She clicked on the Lovely Llama, bouncing around energetically on its own. The random numbers appeared, and Jay looked them up on his phone.

'County General Hospital,' he said.

'Mum!' said Tulip. 'Lovely Llama is Mum!' She looked at Ali, bubbling with excitement. 'One of these other llamas must be Nan-Nan! We can find out where they took her!'

'But which one?' said Ali, annoyed.

There were dozens of llamas lurking about the cartoonish setting. There was Farmer Llama in a hat, Bahama Llama in a flowery shirt, Pyjama Llama and Llamageddon, all bumbling about and being fluffy and cute. 'Why couldn't Nan-Nan just TELL US, so we could use this stupid location app?'

'She knew you'd take it off your phone, if you found out she was tracking you,' said Zac, wisely. 'And she knew you'd need it, one day. She's like the Ninja Nan.'

'We just need to work out which llama is moving somewhere, really fast,' suggested Jay.

'You're lucky you're smart,' said Ali approvingly. 'It almost makes up for being annoying.'

'Aw, back at ya,' said Jay. 'Ali gave a compliment! It's a big moment for me,' and he snapped a photo of them together, with him grinning, and Ali's mouth open in outrage.

'THIS llama is moving the fastest,' said Tulip. 'Check her out. It's like she's on skates.'

'Ooh, that's one of my favourites,' said Ali. 'Llamageddon. Best name. And she's the busiest llama on the app.'

Tulip clicked on her, and they looked up the coordinates. 'She's on the big motorway heading to town,' said Jay. 'We could probably catch up if they pit-stop for food or fuel or something. She's only thirty minutes ahead of us.'

'How are we gonna catch up?' said Ali. 'LeRoi can't drive any faster. I'm not even sure he can drive at all. Stupid haemorrhoids.'

'Hey, the 'rhoids are no joke!' said Tulip. 'Mum had them after us. Said they were agony.'

'We shouldn't have left without his doughnut cushion,' said Zac. 'Any chance they'll have one here?'

Ali rolled her eyes. 'Sure, you'll definitely absolutely find medical comfort supplies in a motorway service station. Between the slushies and the windscreen wiper fluid.'

'Was that a joke?' asked Zac. 'Seriously? I don't know. I've never been in a motorway service station before. This is a first. We stay local or take public transport to keep down our carbon footprint.'

'And what are slushies?' asked Jay.

'Well, I guess it's a big day of firsts for all of us,' said Tulip. 'Never have I ever tracked a nan-napped Nan-Nan using covert llama-location apps.' She squinted into the window. 'Hey, does anyone have any cash?'

'Yep,' said Zac, unexpectedly. 'Your mum gave us each twenty pounds when we left the hospital, to buy some clothes on the way up here, as we were still in jammies.'

'Jammies,' snorted Ali. Even though she said jammies, too.

'But we didn't see anywhere on the way that was selling stuff in organic cotton,' said Jay. 'And I can't wear brand-new clothes that haven't been washed. 'Cause, I've got, you know . . .'

'Allergies,' said Zac and Jay, together. 'Jinx,' they said. 'Argh! Jinx, padlock, 1-2-3.'

'Seriously,' said Ali. 'Do we sound like that when we jinx?'

'Nah, when we do it, it's cute,' said Tulip.

'Cute? That's even worse,' complained Ali, but Tulip talked over her.

'C'mon, guys, we've got some medical work to do in the field,' and she pulled the boys after her. They were jinxed, so they couldn't complain.

When LeRoi came back from the bathroom, the boys and girls had the driver's door open and shouted, 'Ta-da!'

'My doughnut cushion!' he said blissfully, looking at the cushion with a bow. 'How did you find one?'

'We innovated. Put together two of those U-shaped neck cushions, and wrapped it round in toilet paper to make it super-soft-and-strong,' said Tulip, modestly.

'It's unbleached toilet paper,' added Jay. 'Recycled.'

'Yeah, the boys helped too,' said Tulip, generously.

'And we got us all these,' said Zac, holding out a tray of slushies.

'Kids,' said LeRoi, with a tear rolling down his face. 'A slushie! I can't think of the last time I had crushed ice!'

Tulip grinned at Zac. She supposed that they

didn't have a freezer at the Cattery. Catty ran that place like an end-of-the-world apocalyptic bunker.

LeRoi sat down. 'Oh, it's like sitting on a cushion of air!' he said ecstatically.

'Technically, it IS a cushion of air,' said Jay.

'Way to ruin the moment,' said Ali. 'Let's go! We've got Llamageddon to track!'

LeRoi looked confused. 'Llama-geddon?' he said uncertainly.

'We'll catch you up on the way,' said Tulip, kindly.

CHAPTER 20:
NEVER HAVE I EVER

'Ugh, this slushie is definitely NOT no-added-sugar,' complained Jay. 'And it's BLUE! What natural thing is BLUE?'

'The sky?' said Ali. 'The bruise I'm gonna give you if you keep yapping? Never have I ever been stuck in a rolling metal box with such a serious dweeb.'

'I really think we need to establish some boundaries,' said Jay. 'You can't threaten me *and* mock my concerns.'

'Really?' said Ali. 'That will leave me literally nothing to say to you.'

'Never have I ever had a blue slushie on the motorway,' said Zac, dreamily, stirring the mushy remains with the straw. 'This is really nice. Us being together.'

'Hey, not a day out,' said Ali. 'Our Nan-Nan's been kidnapped!'

'You remember our dad got stabbed, right?' said Jay. 'I think stabbing beats nan-napping.'

'NOT a competition, noob,' snapped Ali. 'If it was, we'd win.'

Jay stared at her. 'Never have I ever had such a relentless PAIN in the . . .'

'Please stop bickering,' said Tulip. 'You'll distract LeRoi.'

This was obviously untrue. LeRoi had Tulip's purple headphones on, and was singing loudly to another Elvis song about being nothing but a hound dog, jigging enthusiastically on his cushion, as he roared down the motorway, overtaking all the way down the fast lane. He knew all of the words and did a lot of extravagant gesticulation, sometimes with both hands dangerously off the wheel.

'Well, you'll upset Zac,' she added.

Zac shrugged. 'I just tune it out now,' he said. 'Like white noise.'

'Yeah, sorry,' said Jay, 'I don't know why I even react to Ali any more. It's not her fault she's obnoxious.'

'Puh-leeze,' said Ali. 'You can't even spell obnoxious.'

'Don't need to spell it if I can see it,' he said.

Zac finished his slushie with a final, regretful slurp. 'Never have I ever had anything so teeth-meltingly awesome.' He turned to Tulip. 'Catch me up, here. Why did your nan take you to the Cattery in the first place?'

'It was sort of a job,' admitted Tulip. 'Her team knew something dodgy was going on there.'

'They were right. It was full of sickly old people instead of cats,' said Ali, 'and Catty kept persuading them to give their money to the place.'

'We found that out when Nan-Nan posed as a guest,' said Tulip. 'And then we saw Sprotland. Except that no one knew it was him.'

'Not even him,' said Ali. 'He thought Catty was his mum. Maybe she was.'

'Except she wasn't at the funeral,' mused Tulip. 'TBH, we didn't really have the time to dig deeper into that.'

'We were kinda busy,' said Ali defensively.

'Literally, if we asked all the follow-up questions, we'd never have got anywhere.'

'You don't chat to a choking patient,' nodded Tulip. 'You gotta stick a fist under their ribs and get the steak out first, and ask the questions later.'

'That's why the backroom boys are here,' said Zac, puffing up with pride. 'While you guys were arguing, I was looking up some stuff about the REAL Brian-Sturgeon-Brain-Surgeon and Evelyn Sprotland. Firstly, the Cattery was one of Sturgeon's properties.'

'Abandoned dump in the woods. Looks like it's only been going as a business for a few months,' said Jay, reading the info on Zac's phone.

'No deed of sale. Or rent,' continued Zac. 'Catty's squatting there.'

'And Sprotland?' asked Ali, impressed despite herself. 'Anything on him?'

'Was his mum even called Catty?' asked Tulip.

'Yeah,' said Zac. 'Close enough. She's a Catherine. Least, that's what it says on the adoption paper.'

Tulip gasped. 'Didn't know he was adopted,' she said. 'And we lived with the guy.'

'TBF,' said Ali, 'we lived with him a month before he took his shades off. He was pretty secretive.'

'Hey, look!' said Tulip, checking her phone. 'Llamageddon is hanging out with Lovely Llama!'

'And they're hanging out with loads of Pyjama Llamas,' commented Zac.

'Pyjamas? The hospital!' said Ali. 'That's where Nan-Nan's ended up! But why?'

Both girls were thinking the same thing. What if Nan-Nan had been stabbed too? Like Momo, and Wiggie. Ali reached out for Tulip's hand.

'She'll be alright,' said Zac, giving them both a hug. 'Your nan's the most terrifying person I know.'

'Thanks,' sniffed Tulip.

'Hey, LeRoi,' said Jay, pulling the headphones off his ears. 'We need to get to the hospital! We're on borrowed time.'

'You and me both,' agreed LeRoi, flooring the pedal. 'I'm gonna miss the tea dance with Doris. You only get one dance-chance with Doris. If she picks another partner, I'm history.'

CHAPTER 21:
HOSPITAL HIDE-AND-SEEK

LeRoi screeched up to the hospital so fast that they were all screaming.

'Sorry,' he said. 'Without my haemmorroids getting in the way, I drive like I dance. Like nobody's watching.'

'Hey, we're not complaining,' said Ali. 'Though if I have to hear anyone sing about hound dogs or blue suede shoes again, I might just have to kick them hard in the throat.'

'Or throw up on them,' said Zac, wobbling out of the car. 'Why did I have that slushie? Why, why, why?'

'When we get home, Zac-Zac,' said Jay soothingly, 'I'll get one of Mum's home-made ice-lollies for you.'

'Your mum makes her own lollies?' asked Tulip.

'She does them with fruit tea and sliced peaches. And she adds goji berries for our immune system,' said Zac.

'With no-added-sugar,' said Jay, wistfully.

'Yum,' said Tulip.

'Sarcasm?' whispered Ali.

'I'm not sure,' said Tulip, jumping out of the car after her.

'Thank you for the ride, sir,' said Jay politely to LeRoi. 'Are you coming in? We'll get you a cup of tea before you head home.'

'Oh, no,' said LeRoi, scandalized. 'I can't pay for hospital parking! Why'd you think I'm in the Cattery? We're all there 'cause it's cheap. We're not sick enough for hospital, but we can't afford proper nursing homes and home visits and for people to clean and cook for us.'

'Wait a mo,' said Ali, doubling back from the kerb. 'So how did you find out about Catty's Cattery in the first place?'

'Some doctor-type emailed me after I got

discharged from the hospital, a few weeks back,' said LeRoi, looking nervously at his phone. 'Think I'm in a spot of trouble, someone reported the car stolen. I'd better get it back.'

'Wait, you stole the car?' asked Zac. 'It's not yours?'

'Of course it's not mine. It's the spare Cattery car. What bit of being broke don't you get?' said LeRoi. 'What little we've got, we leave to the Cattery, for putting us up.'

'You stole a car,' said Ali, nodding with a grin. 'Just to help us out. Nice! You're a player.'

LeRoi grinned and high-fived her.

'I've done much more daring stuff,' he said. 'You know, during the war. Whichever one it was.'

'You sure you don't want to come with us and rescue our Nan-Nan?' said Tulip.

'Thanks, kids,' said LeRoi, 'think I've had my share of fun today. Re-lived the good old days. Grand Theft Auto. Blue slushies. Parking illegally.' He was looking nervously around, as a uniform was inspecting cars in the next bay.

'I'm sure Ali could smash up the parking meter so you don't have to pay,' said Jay.

'Sarcasm?' whispered Zac.

'Not really sure,' said Jay.

Tulip gave LeRoi a huge hug. 'You were a hero today,' she said. 'But now we're gonna get our Nan-Nan back!'

'Your mum's in there, right?' said LeRoi, with concern. 'You've got your grown-ups?'

'Definitely,' said Zac, a little sadly. 'Mum's in the ward. So's Dad.'

They waved goodbye, and ran up the ramp into the hospital.

'Where do we go?' asked Zac.

'Emergency, first,' said Ali. 'Gotta check she's not been hurt.'

'So let's go,' said Jay. 'Know our way to that place without a map now.'

'Well, WE know where the secret cookie drawer is,' said Ali, bristling.

'Not everything's a competition,' said Tulip. She stopped, and turned to the boys. 'You go check on your mum and dad, first. We'll meet up later.'

Zac nodded, like he'd wanted to say this for ages. He gave Tulip a grateful hug, and ran up to the stairwell, as the lifts had a long queue. Jay looked uncertain.

'Go on,' said Ali. 'Go see your folks.' She

stepped back. 'But if you give me a hug like Tweedle-dumber I WILL karate chop you in the neck.'

'You're just one big soft marshmallow on the inside,' said Jay, grinning and running after Zac. 'Text me when you've found Llamageddon.'

'Llamageddon?' said a woman's voice. The girls spun around. There was a woman in a trench coat with black curls spilling out from under her hat. Agent Ebony. 'Stay there, girls,' she said in a commanding voice, and she got out her phone.

'We're definitely not girls,' said Ali, spitting extravagantly and hitching up her jeans. 'Been wearing these clothes FOREVER now, that's how gross and boyish we are.'

'Boys don't say they're boyish,' hissed Tulip. 'She's SWAT. D'you think we should trust her?'

''Course not,' hissed Ali. 'Catty's ex-SWAT, who knows who else has been compromised.'

'Tell Silver I've got eyes on them,' Agent Ebony was saying. She beamed at them, showing white and even teeth, and gave them a friendly wave. 'They're looking for Llamageddon. Nope, not on my database, either . . .'

'Maybe she's one of the good guys,' said Tulip.

'No one who spends that much time on dental care could be truly evil.'

'So good guys have good teeth, and bad guys have bad teeth. And alopecia and acne. And a big old scar across the face,' whispered Ali with heavy sarcasm.

'Maybe I've been watching too many superhero flicks,' admitted Tulip. 'Let's go. On three.'

'Splitsies—fire??' said Ali.

'Splitsies—fire,' confirmed Tulip, giving her a tiny fist bump behind her back.

'THREE!' yelled Ali.

'FIRE!' yelled Tulip, and the girls ran in different directions.

'What! Stop!' yelled Agent Ebony, but there was a sudden rush for the fire exits, as people jumped up from the seating area. She saw the girls dash away down two different corridors.

'They're on the move!' she yelled. 'Lost visual. Repeat, lost visual.'

She began running after Ali, just because she had been the mouthier one. 'Find out about Llamageddon,' she screeched into her phone. 'And no, I'm not going to the zoo, you're NOT funny, Amber!'

The girls knew their way around the hospital blindfolded. They'd played hide-and-seek there when Mum had been on call or on night shift, if Nan-Nan couldn't babysit because she was doing her Senior Water Aerobics Training. They knew that there were TWO ways to get to A&E.

Ali found Tulip in the tiny kitchen area in the Paediatric section of A&E, crouching under the window panel.

'Did you lose Agent Ebony?' said Tulip, breathlessly.

'Yep, hid in the storage cupboard and she went right past me, the noob,' said Ali with satisfaction. 'Should've polished her specs, instead of her teeth.'

'Hobnobs or jammie dodgers?' said Tulip, holding out wrapped packets, as she'd already been in the secret biscuit drawer.

'Splitsies, duh,' said Ali, taking half of each. 'Was Nan-Nan here?'

'No,' said Tulip, 'I checked. We're replacing these, OK?' and she munched down the cookies. 'I mean, I'm so relieved, but what now? She could be ANYWHERE!'

She pulled out her phone. It showed Llamageddon, pacing around listlessly in a circle.

'Enclosed space?' suggested Ali. 'Nan-Nan wouldn't be going in circles if she wasn't forced to do that.'

Tulip nodded. She pointed to Lovely Llama, who was now in a different part of the screen, at a cottage surrounded by flowers and cakes. 'Guessing that means Mum's gone home.'

Ali clicked on Llamageddon, but she couldn't get a fix. 'Nan-Nan must have some extra software on her phone that locates better than Google Maps,' she said. 'How're we gonna find her in the hospital?'

'I don't know,' admitted Tulip.

Ali kicked the wall in frustration. 'Aargh!' She chucked her phone on the floor, cracking the screen.

'OMG, calm down,' said Tulip.

'CALM DOWN?' shrieked Ali. 'When, in the HISTORY of NEVER, did anyone CALM DOWN because someone told them to CALM DOWN?!!'

'I said CALM DOWN because there's a possible rogue SWAT agent tailing us, you NOOB!' yelled Tulip. 'Now SHUDDUP!'

There was silence. Ali broke it almost immediately, because she hated letting a silence go unfilled, even when she was wrong.

'You know you *yelled* shuddup,' she said quietly. 'Bit ironic. Bit beside the point. Kinda defeats the object. Of you know . . .'

'Yes,' said Tulip, testily. 'Aware of the irony. Now shush.'

It was too late. They heard Agent Ebony chatting on her phone. 'Not got a visual, but definitely heard them,' she was saying. 'Those girls are NOT subtle. No idea how they're on our books for covert ops. Yes, yes, ear-witnesses all over A&E.'

'Great,' whispered Tulip. 'We still don't know where Nan-Nan is, and now we've gotta escape A&E.'

'My queens?' said a weak voice.

'MOMO!' mouthed the girls in unison. They peeked around, and saw him in a hospital wheelchair, looking quizzically about. He was carrying a box of chocolates, which he was wheeling towards the little kitchen. It had a Thank You note taped to the top, and was addressed to the A&E staff.

'Aw,' said Tulip, 'Momo's the best.'

'He deffo has the best timing,' said Ali. 'Come on, the do-gooding-cab-jockey's our ticket outta here.'

'Hide in plain sight?' suggested Tulip. She was already peeling off plastic aprons from the roll in the kitchen, and snapping on a mask and hairnet.

'Hey, big bro,' said Ali brightly a few minutes later, jumping out and taking the handles of Momo's wheelchair. She hissed, 'Play along.'

Momo grinned, showing his blindingly white teeth, as Tulip popped out too.

'We were just looking for you,' she said. 'Love playing hide-and-seek, ready or not here we come!'

They strolled confidently down the corridor.

'We're gonna pretend you said something funny,' said Ali, and she started laughing her head off.

The SWAT agent was on the phone, looking under beds and in cupboards.

'What are you doing, madam?' challenged one of the nurses.

'I've lost my friend's grandkids,' said Agent Ebony crossly. She was looking for two kids who were hiding, so she ignored the noisy, laughing kids in infection-control aprons, wheeling their big brother out of the department.

Until the last moment, when Ali made the mistake of looking back, smugly. Just as the lift doors were closing.

'Ready or not, here we GO!' she called out, with a little wave.

'Hey, you!' Agent Ebony yelled, racing up towards them, but it was too late. Ali gave a triple bow as the doors shut on her face.

Tulip had hit the top floor button. 'Momo!' she squealed, hugging him. 'So glad you're alright!'

'It is always a delight, my queens,' bowed Momo. But then he frowned. 'Are you aware your mother has left for the day? Where is your Nan-Nan?'

'That's the million dollar question,' said Ali. 'Some insane woman's kidnapped her. And we think she's brought her here.'

'Ah,' said Momo, as though this was perfectly normal news. 'And is that the same insane woman you were evading most mightily in Emergency?'

'Nope, different insane woman,' said Tulip. 'She's called Catty. From the Cattery.' She showed him a shot on her phone. 'Any chance you've seen her?' She knew there was no chance. Ali thought so too, as she rolled her eyes.

They were both stunned, when Momo nodded. 'I have certainly seen this lady,' he said. Frowning a mini-mountain range. It was the closest to cross they had ever seen him. Tulip didn't think he even knew how to frown.

'Where?' said Ali.

'In my cab,' said Momo. 'That is the woman who I collected on your last day of school. She asked to drive to your road. She wrapped herself up in many layers and a most heinous hat on the way. Fancy dress, she said. We waited, as she said her friend was not yet home.'

'That's the woman who stabbed you!' said Tulip. '*Catty* stabbed you!'

'So she must've stabbed Wiggie, too!' said Ali.

'And now she's got Nan-Nan!' said Tulip. 'Momo, we've gotta get to her.'

The doors opened on the fifth floor.

'I think,' said Momo, indicating his injured leg, 'you have NOT got to get to her. I think you should possibly go as far away from her as possible. I will be calling your mother.'

'Fine, you do that,' said Ali, pushing him out of the lift. She waved as the door closed.

'Think,' said Tulip, trying not to feel guilty about poor Momo ditched on the fifth floor.

'An enclosed space in the hospital where no one would go. That's where they've hidden Nan-Nan.'

'Operating theatre?' said Ali. 'Any clinical cubicle or side room? Mortuary?' She looked with annoyance at her phone. The boys were messaging.

'SEVENTH FLOOR, STAIRCASE C. NOW!'

Tulip looked at her phone too. 'But there's no seventh floor? At least, we've never been there with Mum.'

'Noobs,' said Ali. 'Let's just go to Staircase C before Agent Ebony mops them up.'

'Aw,' said Tulip, 'you're looking out for them.'

'Nope,' said Ali, 'I'm just cleaning the scene.' Tulip was still grinning at her. 'Stop it!' she said.

They got off at the sixth floor, as the lift didn't go any higher, and ran down the corridor to the Staircase C sign.

'WHERE R U?' texted Tulip. 'NO SEVENTH FLOOR.'

'STAIRS. HURRY,' Zac messaged back.

The girls shrugged, and took the stairs.

'If there's not a secret passageway at the end of this,' complained Ali, 'I'm gonna burn those boys so bad.'

At the top of the stairs was the shiny patient-accessible double door to the sixth floor. That was it. Except for a small service door, with no handle, but just a keypad, which had a 'No Entry' sign on it.

'Fire exit?' said Tulip, tapping it nervously. It didn't open.

'I'm guessing this might be one of those motion-sensored doors,' said Ali, thoughtfully.

'Motion-sensored?' said Tulip, and watched Ali stepping back to make a running jump at the door.

'Hi-yah!' yelled Ali, kicking it hard, and it trembled, but it didn't open.

'Might need a bit more motion,' said Tulip. 'On three! One-two-three!' And they kicked together.

The door shuddered and opened. It was how they used to open the doctors' mess door in the hospital, to get to the TV and table tennis, as Mum's card never worked for it.

They looked in wonder, as beyond the door, was a narrow flight of stairs, lined with flimsy plasterboard walls, with a sign which said, 'Seventh Floor. Administrative Offices.'

'Wow,' said Tulip. 'A hidden passageway.'

'It's like finding Platform nine and three quarters,' said Ali. 'Or Narnia at the back of the wardrobe.'

They heard the boys at the top of the stairs.

'Tulip? Ali?' whispered Jay. 'Come on up.'

The girls went up, and found them crouching at the top of the stairs. 'Why are we here?' asked Tulip, reasonably enough.

'Your Nan-Nan,' said Zac. 'We went to see Mum, and she's not been well, and they haven't been giving her the right meds at the right time, and she'd tried to complain, but it was impossible, because of budget cutbacks. Dad said they'd fired the patient complaints team, and their office was *deserted* and *empty*.'

'And we thought, if we really wanted to hide someone in the hospital . . .'

'You'd hide them in an empty office on the admin floor!' said Ali. 'Oh sorry, was that your big finish?'

'It was,' said Jay. 'But you can have it. That's cool.'

'Genius,' said Tulip, pushing open the door, and peering around the corridor. 'These admin offices will be empty all weekend, and after

5 pm.'

'Yeah, yeah,' said Ali. 'Backroom boys strike again, and all that. But don't high-five until we find Nan-Nan.'

They carefully went through the door, and crawled along the cheaply-carpeted corridor, which was lined with makeshift offices divided by plasterboard and plastic frames. All of the cubicles were identical and windowless. It was the blandest maze ever.

'Seriously, if you were lost in this place, you'd never get out,' said Jay. 'It's like death by beige.'

'Mum says corporations are evil,' said Zac, looking in horror at the miles of plasterboard.

'TBH, your mum says sugar is evil, too. And gluten,' said Ali. 'And pizza, probably . . .'

'Oh no,' said Zac. 'Mum would never mock ethnic food.'

'Shush,' said Tulip. She paused and leaned against the plasterboard partition, which wobbled gently. 'Can you hear that?'

There was a snuffling, and a scuffling. An icky, sicky smell.

'OMG,' squeaked Jay. 'They've got MICE here. I HATE mice.'

'You and your allergies,' scoffed Ali. 'If that's

a mouse, it really stinks.'

'It's not a mouse,' said Tulip. 'Look!'

Emerging from behind the overflowing beige recycling bins, was a black shadow. A fat black shadow. Stalking smugly as though she had just strolled out from an exploding building.

'Witchy!' said Tulip.

'We seriously can't get rid of her,' said Ali, grinning. 'She's what smells so bad.'

'Seriously, how is she here?' said Jay. 'She wasn't with us, was she?'

'Nope,' said Zac. 'And there was only one other car that came here from the Cattery. The one that Catty was driving.'

Witch gave up playing it cool, and after snaking around Ali's calves, leapt up into Tulip's arms.

'Clever, clever Witchy!' said Tulip. 'She must've got in the boot with Nan-Nan, with the big bag of trash. She's like the Ninja Cat!'

'Well, you know what this means . . .' said Jay.

'We're looking in the right place!' they all said together. 'Jinx! Jinx, padlock, 1-2-3!'

They were stuck in silence. And Witch, shaking her sleek head at their silliness, leapt out of Tulip's arms, and started strolling down the narrow corridors, sniffing some bits of rubbish strewn along the way. Tulip recognized the fishy smell from the trash bag, and realized Nan-Nan had probably scattered bits for them to follow. She indicated with a head jerk that they should follow, and Ali rolled her eyes, like that much was obvious. Zac started to go after them, but Jay pulled him back, and texted rapidly.

'We should wait here and watch the doors! Only one way out of this place! Then they can't escape with her.'

Ali and Tulip nodded. Surprised by how smart this was.

The girls crept after Witch, going deeper into the plasterboard maze, following the rubbish like a breadcrumb trail through the woods. Finally, they came to a boarded-up room. The Patient Complaints office. There was a spider dangling happily from the handle. There was someone whimpering inside.

It wasn't Nan-Nan.

It was Manny.

CHAPTER 22:
BONES AND THE DUMMY

'Let's go, Mumsy, please let's go! And let HER go. I never agreed to kidnap old ladies! You told me I'd be running a nice hotel for them. For impoverished invalids.'

'Oh do shut up, Manny,' said Catty. 'I've told you lots of things. If I had to make sure they were all true, that would be far too much like hard work.'

'And why are we even here?' whined Manny.

The girls looked through the slats in the blinds. He was huddled into a ball in the corner of the office, hugging his knees in distress. They couldn't see Nan-Nan, just the edge of her wheelchair. And Catty was striding up and down the office. She'd found some hospital clogs for her large feet. She was holding a syringe and waving it around psychotically.

'For supplies!' said Catty, showing him the needle. 'I need to decide what to do with the sweet little granny here. I don't know who she's told.'

'Who she's told?' said Manny. 'About what?'

'You're getting a bit mouthy, Manny,' said Catty. 'You're asking a lot of questions that don't concern you. You're Manny Gers, the manager. That's all you do. That's all you are.'

'Is that who I am?' asked Manny. 'I'm suddenly not so sure any more. I'm not so sure who you are, either.'

'Really,' said Catty, with interest. 'I think you need another dose, my dear. Your medication is running low.'

The girls heard a furious noise, muffled by something.

'At least take her gag off,' said Manny. 'I'm worried she'll choke. And no one will hear her scream.'

'Fine,' snapped Catty, tapping the syringe. 'If she does, I can shut her up. And I need to know what she knows.'

The girls watched Nan-Nan's wheelchair roll into view. Her eyes were blazing, and she shot Catty a look that could have fried her.

Catty pulled off the gag, and Nan-Nan coughed right into her over-made-up face.

'Oh, I'm sorry, dear,' said Nan-Nan with heavy sarcasm, 'that was impolite.' She smiled, sweetly. It was even more chilling. 'Did you have a question for me?'

'What do you know?' snapped Catty. 'Who have you told?'

Nan-Nan sighed. 'That was two questions, dear. I thought you'd have mastered counting.' She looked at Catty shrewdly, 'But then, you were always keen on two for the price of one, weren't you? Two-faced, like I said at the Cattery. Two identities at a time?'

'What's she talking about, Mumsy?' said Manny, fearfully.

'Fine!' said Catty, through gritted teeth. 'One question. What do you know?'

'I think the question,' said Nan-Nan, 'is what does HE know?' She nodded towards Manny, who curled more tightly into his ball, like a child in deep distress.

'Mumsy knows best . . . Mumsy knows best . . .' he was muttering to himself.

Ali nudged Tulip. 'This is really upsetting him.'

Tulip nodded, surprised by her twin's concern. 'It's not nice, we have to help him, too.'

'Nothing,' spat Catty. 'Manny knows nothing.' She spun round, as she heard a siren blaring. An ambulance was coming into the hospital. And then the heavy thudding of chopper blades, as a helicopter swung round the sky towards the helipad.

'Is that your back-up? How did you call them? I've got your phone right here!' And she waved the phone at Nan-Nan.

'You're paranoid, dear,' said Nan-Nan. 'This is a general hospital, remember? Very sick people get flown in and driven in all the time. There are people here with bigger issues than your piddling little plots!'

'My little plots put two of those people in this hospital!' retorted Catty.

'Yes, well I'm sure *your* mother's proud,' said Nan-Nan.

Catty's eyes went wide and wild at this. 'DON'T mention my mother,' she hissed. And she held the needle high, uncoiling like a snake getting ready to strike. 'A little dose of THIS will get you talking . . .'

'NOOOO!!!!' screamed Tulip and Ali, and they burst into the room, leaping for Catty. But Manny had leapt for her at the same time, and they all bumped into each other. Leaving Catty enough space to get behind Nan-Nan. Brandishing the needle.

Tulip was breathing heavily, from the floor, taking in the scene. The Patient Complaints office was admin hell, full of brown boxes, overflowing files and store-room junk. There was a desk in the corner, where someone had parked a broken skeleton, hanging on a drip stand beside an educational resuscitation dummy, that was sitting at the desk with her head in her hands.

'Someone's got a sense of humour here,' said Ali, pushing herself up. 'That's just waiting for a caption competition. Bones and the Dummy.'

'Bit less funny from where I'm sitting,' said Nan-Nan, pleasantly.

Catty's needle was pressed against the skin of her neck. Nan-Nan didn't seem surprised to see them.

'You!' bellowed Catty, glowering at the

girls, eyes wide with recognition. 'You! Again! Wherever your pesky granny is, you always have to be scampering around too, like pesky puppies!' She shook her head furiously. 'Can't believe I didn't recognize you when you were playing Operation!'

'Sorry, have we met?' said Ali, disdainfully.

Tulip looked confused. 'We worked out that you knew Nan-Nan,' she said, 'but how do you know us?'

'Boys?' said Manny, staring at Ali and Tulip in confusion. It was the first time he'd looked at them properly without the caps and curly wigs. 'Are you *girls*?'

'Oh just shut up, Leslie,' snapped Catty. Her voice was completely different. And chillingly familiar. 'Do you have to say stupid things all the time? Isn't it enough just *being* stupid? Why didn't I get a T-shirt saying, *I'm with stupid*? Best day of my life when they split us up!'

'Leslie?' said Manny. 'Wasn't that . . . my name, once?'

The twins looked at each other. They'd finally worked it out. The Evil Twin and the Not-Evil Twin.

'So Manny's not Evelyn Sprotland,' said Ali,

slowly.

Tulip stared hard at the tall, horrible woman in oversized shades holding a loaded syringe to her Nan-Nan's throat.

'Nope. Catty is,' she said.

CHAPTER 23:
THE BROTHERS SPROTLAND

'Well, the cat's out of the bag, *Catty*,' said Nan-Nan, pushing Catty-Sprotland's hand away. 'I'm sure you'll be wanting to monologue, but I think that the girls should be taking your poor brother away. This episode seems to have quite upset him.'

'His brother,' nodded Tulip, looking between Catty and Manny.

'Oh yes,' said Nan-Nan. 'Remarkable resemblance. Not twins, though. Manny the Manager is actually Leslie, Evelyn Sprotland's little brother. Evelyn's been controlling him for months . . .'

'With medication! Just like you did with Mum,' said Ali. 'That's evil, Evelyn.'

'And we thought you were dead,' said Tulip, sorrowfully, shaking her head. 'Not cool, Evelyn.'

'Hoped you were dead, more like,' corrected Ali.

'So, who knew that Evelyn Sprotland had a brother?' asked Tulip.

'Just me. We were separated when I was three,' said Manny-Leslie, shaking his head violently. He was shuddering, shaking and sweating. It seemed as though his medication was finally wearing off. 'Adopted separately. The social services thought it was best. He kept . . . experimenting on me, apparently.'

'My first subject,' said Evelyn Sprotland. 'Leslie would've had a place in the history books if he'd shut up and done what he was told.'

Leslie stood up furiously, fists balled. 'You JERK, Evelyn. Thirty years later and you're *still* experimenting on me. What have you done?'

Sprotland did something unexpected. He laughed. The girls didn't think they'd heard him laugh before. It wasn't pleasant. He gave them a handclap, and took off his scarf and his rock-hard wig. He tore off a fake nose, and began wiping his face, and the thick plastic make-up practically peeled off.

'I've done something brilliant, little brother. I set up Catty's Cattery with the money and property I stole from Brian Sturgeon the Brain Surgeon.'

'Who?' said Leslie.

'That was my last victim of identity theft,' said Evelyn impatiently. 'Don't make me recap! I hate recapping. But I've made millions, taking money from the poorly and the elderly. And all the paperwork, went through YOU . . .'

'What?' said Leslie.

'So YOU'RE the criminal, my little brother, not ME. I'm a ghost, and I'm going to get away with it, too . . .'

'No you're not,' said Ali fiercely. 'We're here. We found you. Really easily.'

'Yeah!' said Tulip. 'We just followed a trail of TRASH and it led us straight to you!'

Evelyn laughed. 'You think I can't handle my over-medicated little bother, two children and an old lady tied to a wheelchair?' He gestured wildly around the room, towards the dummy and the skeleton. 'You think *they're* gonna help you?'

'The SWAT team are here, too,' said Tulip. 'They're following us upstairs.'

'Hmm, well first, that's a big fat lie,' said Evelyn. 'Secondly, SWAT are going to be completely discredited, as I've been busy framing them expertly for my various crimes. And thirdly, by the time anyone gets here, you'll be dead and I'll be gone!'

'Dead?' said Leslie, looking with horror at the twins. He moved in front of them protectively.

'Oh don't be so dramatic, Evelyn,' said Nan-Nan. 'The only thing you're murdering today is some derivative super-villain material.'

'Yeah, he just doesn't have the delivery,' said Ali, edging closer to the desk in the corner.

'Or the timing,' said Tulip, moving with her.

'You've always underestimated me, Ruby,' hissed Evelyn to Nan-Nan. 'You think I won't do it? The only people who know that Evelyn Sprotland is alive and at large are in this room!'

His face, with the half-mask of Catty on it, looked psychotic and terrifying.

'Oh yes, I'll do it,' he hissed. 'I can DO FOR YOU!'

Tulip shivered, remembering how Wiggie's

attacker had said exactly that on the video clip.

'I'LL SHOW YOU ALL!' His arms were raised manically in the air.

'Get out, girls,' said Nan-Nan, calmly. 'RUN!'

'NO!' said Ali and Tulip, together. They didn't jinx. They were stunned with fear, as Evelyn made a fist of his raised hand, with the syringe, and brought it swinging down towards Nan-Nan.

And then a lot of things happened at once.

Someone else shouted, 'JINX. JINX, PADLOCK, 1-2-3!'

Nan-Nan's biceps bulged and she crashed her wheelchair sideways towards the ground, knocking Evelyn hard in the hip, so he went sprawling across the plastic flooring.

Ali grabbed the skeleton and smashed it over Evelyn, so bones crashed across the floor.

Tulip knocked the resus dummy on to Evelyn, hitting the arrest button so that it sparked with a fake heart attack, jerking with electricity on top of him.

And Zac and Jay came bowling into the room, with LeRoi on a mobility scooter, knocking the paperwork to the ground, covering Evelyn and the floor in a snow of printed A4 paper, which gently drifted down.

The Patient Complaints office looked like a snow globe.

'Now this,' said Ali, standing up and dusting herself off, 'is something for the caption competition.'

'And that,' said Tulip, hugging the boys, 'was great timing! You distracted him just long enough for us to bring him down.'

'Ruby?' said LeRoi. 'Long time no undercover crime. Thought you'd retired?'

'LeRoi?' said Nan-Nan, from the ground. 'Thought you'd died.'

'Hahaha,' said LeRoi, hopping off the mobility scooter, and helping her right the wheelchair. 'Not dead yet. Felt a bit guilty leaving the kids. And then I saw one of the SWAT girls stomping crossly about in A&E, and knew something was going down.'

'We like to be called WOMEN, LeRoi, not girls,' sniffed Nan-Nan. 'And no one needed your wrinkly wisecracks to save the day, I was doing just fine without you.'

'Yeah, TBH, you guys just made a mess in here,' said Ali. 'We completely had him.'

The paper had settled, and they looked around the destroyed office.

'Hold on,' said Tulip. 'Where's Manny? I mean, Leslie?'

'Who's Leslie?' said Jay. 'The manager bloke is on the floor, there.' He pointed next to Nan-Nan's wheelchair.

Aghast, the girls stared, and saw Leslie groaning on the floor, exactly where they thought Evelyn had been trapped.

'Aargh!' shrieked Ali. 'You lost him! We had him, and you gave him a paper storm cover to make an escape . . .'

'We were trying to help,' said Zac. 'I mean, it looked like he wanted to kill you . . .'

'I'M GONNA KILL YOU,' said Ali, running for the boys, held back only by Tulip.

'Chillax,' said Tulip. 'There's only one exit, remember?'

'And the boys had it covered,' said Ali. 'But they're here!'

'We piled up a filing cabinet and a load of stuff there,' said Jay, smugly. 'There's no way out.'

'Yeah, this place is a real fire hazard,' said Zac. 'You wouldn't want to have a birthday party here. Any naked flames and you'd be toast . . .'

He stopped talking, and turned urgently to the others. 'The FIRE ESCAPE!'

CHAPTER 24:
FIRE AND FALL

'Stop,' said Nan-Nan, as they were racing out of the door. 'Leave Evelyn Sprotland to SWAT, he's armed and dangerous!'

'Sorry, Nan-Nan,' said Tulip, running back to drop a kiss on Nan-Nan's head. 'You're all tied up. Not letting that lunatic on the loose. He already put Momo and Wiggie in hospital.'

'HE's the one!' said Jay, looking out of the open door in horror.

'He stabbed our dad!' said Zac. His face twisted into an expression the girls had never seen on him before. Vengeful fury. 'Oh, it is

ON!' he shouted, like a war cry.

They raced out the door. 'We're gonna find that fire escape!' yelled Jay.

Nan-Nan sighed. 'OK, go save those boys,' she said. 'They're too nice for this. Gotta feeling that their organic cooking talent isn't going to help them against a psychotic Sprotland.'

'I'd help, but the mobility scooter is stuck in the paperwork,' said LeRoi.

Nan-Nan looked crossly at LeRoi. 'No-one wanted your help, LeRoi! Then or now. Haven't you got a bad showbiz impression to be doing somewhere?'

'Sorry, Ruby,' said LeRoi. 'I did bring the girls here, though. You know, I do miss the old team. Not the action. More the company.'

'You're sorry? Really?' said Nan-Nan. She gave half a smile. 'Don't just stand there gawping, LeRoi! Untie me! I've gotta screw on my legs.'

Ali was looking impatiently at Tulip. 'Come on!' she said, dragging her out of the door, and down the plasterboard corridors. 'No follow-up questions!'

'They definitely have history,' said Tulip. 'Did you think they just used to work together. Or date?'

'What's the difference between ignorance and indifference?' said Ali, over her shoulder, as they ran.

'Don't know, don't care,' said Tulip. 'Oh, OK, gotcha.'

They drew to a halt as they came to a T-junction in the maze.

'Splitsies?' suggested Ali.

'I'm not sure,' said Tulip. 'We don't know our way round this floor at all. Divided means defenceless.'

They heard a smug meow behind them, and Witchy slid up, with feathers in her mouth.

'Oh, not now, stupid cat,' huffed Ali. 'Don't care how much bird for breakfast you scavenged.'

'Great timing, clever cat,' grinned Tulip. 'Don't you see? She found the fire escape!' She petted Witch, and pulled the feathers out of her teeth. 'Go on, Witchy, show us where you got these!'

The cat turned her back on Ali with slouching disdain, and then began racing down the right corridor, like a fat, black streak.

'Good Witchy!' said Tulip, and they followed her around the curving maze, and stopped, as they came to an open window, with the fire hose wound beside it. Jay and Zac were already there, hanging out uncertainly.

'That daddy-stabbing jerk climbed down there!' said Jay, shaking his fist out of the window.

They could see Evelyn Sprotland, his wig and scarf back on, leaning casually over the fire escape on the floor below, like he was enjoying the view. Nothing but a thin rail between him and a six-floor drop to concrete. The helicopter was circling noisily overhead.

'Oh beans and chickpeas,' said Zac, staring down. 'We can't follow him down there. He's pulled back the ladder.'

'Why did you do it?' shrieked Jay, down to him. 'Why'd you stab our dad? And Momo?'

They heard maniacal laughter, but Evelyn didn't even turn round towards them. 'I saw them with Minnie. I knew they were her friends. And I was going to hurt her, the way she hurt me. I saw her HUG them!'

'OMG,' said Tulip. 'Are you STILL jealous of Mum? You were crushing on her at thirteen, get over it already!'

'Get over it!' cackled Evelyn. 'You've cost me

my latest and greatest scheme, you brats! You cost me my Nobel, when you cured the Sleeping Sickness I unleashed! You cost me millions, by uncovering Catty's Cattery! I'm NEVER going to get over this!'

And then they saw it, an open flame. A spray of stinking oil dousing Catty's clothes. And suddenly, Evelyn Sprotland went up in flames.

'NO, stop,' yelled Tulip.

'Oh, that's horrible, we've got to save him!' shrieked Zac. He began yanking at the looped fire hose next to the exit.

Ali and Jay were silent. As silent as Evelyn, who was bizarrely making no sound at all.

'Do we, though?' asked Nan-Nan, who had caught up with them on her fake legs.

LeRoi was there, climbing off the scooter. Tulip and Zac blinked at her with big wet eyes. They both held out the fire hose to her.

'Oh, alright, then,' she groused, making an expert knot around her waist with the fire hose. 'We'll do the old Fire-Fall, LeRoi!'

He nodded, and she climbed out of the building and swung down to the fire escape. LeRoi took charge of unravelling the hose to let her down, like it was something he'd done lots of times before, and she landed neatly, just behind Evelyn. She yanked off the hose and sprayed Evelyn Sprotland with a jet of foamy water, dousing the flames instantly.

Except that Evelyn went flying over the edge of the thin metal bar with the water pressure, falling down the six floors to the car park below.

And cracked open.

It wasn't Evelyn Sprotland. It was the dummy.

'Wait a minute,' said Tulip. 'Where did he go?'

They watched, as four ambulances left the hospital, racing to different corners of the city. And the helicopter shot back up into the sky, chopping the air furiously.

'Anywhere,' said Ali, staring at the ambulances, at the helicopter. She shook her fist furiously. He could have made his escape with any of them. 'Evelyn Sprotland could've gone anywhere.'

CHAPTER 25:
NEW FACE

'Nice of you to have put me up for the night,' said Leslie, tidying away the breakfast things. 'Nice to be finally discharged. But I really need to be heading home, now. It's a long way, and Mumsy will be wondering where I am.'

'Mumsy?' said Tulip uncertainly.

Poor Leslie had been in the hospital's Intensive Care unit for a week, getting the dodgy medication filtered out of his blood. She wasn't sure he'd fully recovered.

'Manny, I mean, Leslie, you know that . . .'

'Oh, I don't mean that crazed brother of

mine,' said Leslie. 'I mean my real Mumsy. And my girlfriend. I think they're going to be a bit miffed with me for going AWOL with Evelyn for so long. It's a busy season, around half term, we run a campsite in the country.'

'Oh, so you really are a sort of manager,' said Ali.

'Maybe that's what gave Evelyn the idea,' shrugged Leslie. 'Hadn't seen him for years. And I vaguely remember that he turned up a few months ago with a box of chocolates. Wearing shades and a stupid hat. After that, it's a bit of a blur.'

'TBH, all hats are stupid,' said Ali. 'That's how he got Mum. He snuck some dodgy meds in her chocolates. She ate the lot.'

'But they were really nice ones, munchkin,' said Mum, finishing off her breakfast doughnut. 'I'm only human.'

'I feel bad about all your friends at Catty's Cattery,' said Leslie. 'Hope they don't feel abandoned.'

'Don't worry about that,' said LeRoi, pouring himself another coffee. 'Doris is looking after our people. And the SWAT team are sorting out new residential spots. And getting everyone their money back.'

'But you're very welcome to the campsite for your next hols,' said Leslie. 'On the house. The pool has a slide. And I lead the Swim Disco.'

'Sounds fun,' grinned Ali. 'Never been camping.'

'Aw, thanks, Leslie,' said Tulip. 'Guess we better get to school.' She went to hug Mum. 'See you later, alligator!'

'In a while, crocodiles,' said Mum, kissing her and Ali.

'I'll walk you in,' said LeRoi. 'I'm loving this new mobility scooter. I can get anywhere, now. As long as I've got my doughnut cushion.'

On the walk down to school, they were accompanied by Witchy, who then ran off to hiss viciously at the Robo-Cat, placed on sentry duty at the vet's at the end of the street. Witch still thought she was the alpha, especially as she'd helped save the day with her bit of bird-murder at the hospital.

'So,' said LeRoi, 'did your Nan-Nan ever mention me?'

'Nope,' said Ali, bluntly.

'Sorry,' said Tulip, more kindly. 'Were you friends?'

'Oh no, not really friends,' said LeRoi. 'Friends are nice to each other. But she saved my life a few times. In the war. In the old country.'

'Which old country?' asked Tulip.

'Which war?' asked Ali.

'I forget,' he said blithely.

'That's what Nan-Nan always says,' said Tulip, shrewdly. 'You worked together, didn't you? You said you had a trench coat. And that you left your water aerobics team.'

'Didn't think you were paying attention,' grinned LeRoi.

'And you said you had a big gig as a female impersonator. You meant you were on the SWAT team!' said Ali. 'Duh!'

'I'm sorry you had to leave,' said Tulip. 'Was it 'cause they found out you were a guy?'

'Yeah. My bad for lying to them,' said LeRoi. 'I really wanted to get on the team. Best rogue agents I ever worked with.'

'Knew you were rogue the moment you tried to hustle me in a board game with a fake tremor,' commented Ali.

'You know,' said LeRoi, 'I heard what Sprotland said. About never getting over his first love. I sort of get it.'

'First love?' said Ali. 'You don't mean, Nan-Nan?'

'See you later, alligators,' said LeRoi, grinning, as Nan-Nan's Nan-mobile was approaching.

'I came to check in on Minnie,' said Nan-Nan, winding down the window. 'Come on, LeRoi, I'll give you a ride back.'

'I've been thinking about calling myself Leroy, now,' he said, rolling his scooter inside the car. 'Or maybe just Roy.'

'Well that's just stupid,' said Nan-Nan. 'Roy's a rubbish name for an Elvis impersonator. You'll never win the World Championships again with that on the leader board.' And she waved the girls goodbye.

The girls carried on walking, and saw the boys waiting for them at the gates.

'I don't get how Nan-Nan has any game at all,' said Ali. 'All these people seem to like her. But she's just so mean to everyone.'

Tulip said nothing, and just grinned.

'What?' complained Ali. 'What does that mean?'

'I literally said nothing,' said Tulip. 'But it's just funny. Do you remember how you said you were gonna kill the boys? And they still like you.

For some reason.'

'Humph,' said Ali. When they reached Jay and Zac she made a big deal of smiling and asking how their dad was.

'Yeah, he's back in action,' said Zac, surprised. 'Mum's back home, too, now. Thanks.'

'Why're you here so early?' asked Tulip.

'Surprise for you,' said Jay. 'Come in and see.'

They went down the corridor towards their classroom, and there was a shelf outside, with all the girls' artwork from last term.

'Aww,' said Tulip, 'you came back and saved it! We thought it would get chucked out.'

'More than that,' said Zac, and he showed them a sign, with a 'Ta-da!'

'The Ali and Tulip gallery,' read Ali. 'Oh, wow, that's so . . .'

'That's so sweet,' said Tulip, firmly, giving Ali a hard look so she wouldn't misbehave.

'I thought about what you said, about how you never got to keep your art, and you had nowhere to put it,' said Zac. 'So this is just for the week. But your mum can come and see it when she's off. And we've put a photo slideshow together. So you'll always have it, even if it gets recycled.'

'Wow,' said Ali. 'You guys are gonna be great parents one day.'

'Sarcasm?' asked Jay.

Ali shook her head, and she held out her arms. And then she stepped forward heavily and hugged them both.

'OMG, Ali's hugging us,' said Jay. 'Quick, take a picture, I want proof!'

'Shh,' said Zac. 'Make a big deal, and she'll chop us both in the necks.'

They all walked into Mr Ofu's class together. They were the first kids there.

'So, what about Sprotland?' asked Jay. 'Guess the guy is still at large.'

Ali laughed. 'What about him? He's a ghost. Dude's long gone. Don't care about his petty plotting. He can't show his stupid-stupid face anywhere around us, or Mum, or the hospital, or anywhere ever again!'

Zac looked worried. 'Unless,' he said.

He looked at Tulip, who nodded, as though she agreed with him.

'Unless,' said Tulip carefully, 'he gets a NEW stupid-stupid face.'

They were all quiet for a moment, and then Ali shrugged and smiled, 'No biggie if he does.

We outnumber him. We've got back-up. We've got each other.'

She was being absolutely sincere for a moment. It kind of took them all by surprise, especially Ali.

And then Tulip played back what Ali had said, she'd been surreptitiously recording it.

'Aw, that's beautiful, Ali!' she grinned. '*We've got each other!* Now THAT'S the twinspirational line that's going on my cat poster! And it came out of you! Your voice'll be on my blog FOREVER!'

'What! Don't you dare!' shrieked Ali, back to being Ali. 'Delete that! Delete it now!' and she chased Tulip around the classroom desks. In full Ali explode-mode.

Tulip was laughing hysterically, running away, holding her phone just out of reach, re-playing the clip, squealing, 'HashtagAliCat!' and 'HashtagAliCares!'

Ali shrieked and threw her own beeping phone at Tulip, furiously. 'No, No, NO! You are not doing this to me! OMG this is SO typical of you!'

Mr Ofu arrived at the classroom, with his rolling luggage, and still in his holiday shorts, looking bewildered. 'Shouldn't we stop them?' he asked the boys.

'Home-made cookies, sir?' said Zac, avoiding the question, handing over a box.

'Agent Cocoa and Agent Brownie,' said a stern voice from Ali's phone, spinning on the plastic flooring. 'Agent Silver here. We've got a job. Report tonight at Agent Ruby's for Senior Water Aerobics Training briefing. Silver out.'

Ali and Tulip stopped in their tracks, eyes wide. They spotted Mr Ofu, gaping at the door, and sat down promptly at their desks.

'Someone going to explain to me what's going on?' asked Mr Ofu.

Tulip and Ali and Zac and Jay looked at each other. One of those silent twin conversations, with the head-tilt and half-nod, except it was four ways, and for once they were all in total agreement.

'Sorry, sir, not even gonna try,' said Ali, with a grin.

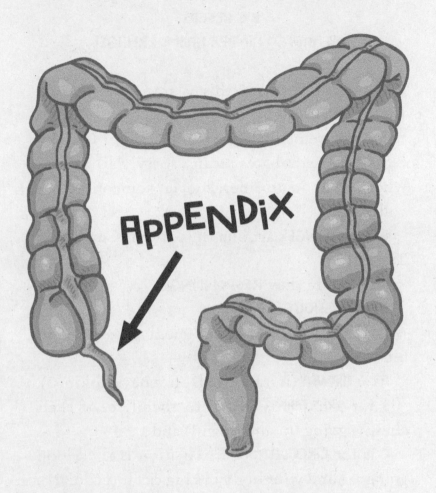

APPENDIX

Tulip says: An appendix is an extra bit at the end of a book. It is also an extra bit dangling off your gut.

EMERGENCY TWINTERVENTiON!
BiG BLEEDS
OR HOW TO HiNDER HAEMORRHAGE!

Hey, I'm Tulip, and this is my #Mini-Medix Blog! 😊 👊

Do you remember the **DRS ABC** blog? Quick recap (my sister hates recaps, sorry, Ali). It's what you do in an emergency, if someone's collapsed.

D is for **DANGER** around the patient (Cars! Fire! Tigers!),

R is for are they **RESPONDiNG,**

S is for **SHOUT** for help.

And then the **ABC** is the medical assessment bit:

A for **AIRWAY** (is it blocked? Are they choking?),

B for **BREATHING** (listen to them! see if their chest is going up and down!) and

C is for **CiRCULATiON.** Circulation is the blood going around your body in a big circle (geddit?!). That's what this blog is about.

And that's the problem with a big bleed, which is what happened to our friend, Momo. He was stabbed in a major artery, which is a big pipe delivering the blood around your body, and he sprung a serious leak.

Why is that a bad thing? Well, the blood's meant to go round-and-round your body, and if you let it out, there's not enough to get to your organs. Which is a BAD thing. You can die from a big bleed, that's what haemorrhage means.

So, if you're first on the scene, and someone's bleeding, once you've checked that their airway and breathing is OK, your job is to STOP THE LEAK. The best way to do that is with pressure —when I saw that Momo had sprung a leak out of the back of his knee, I just jammed my own knee really hard over the wound, so no more blood could come out. If I'd had bigger hands, I could have pressed on it, and that would have worked too.

Sounds pretty basic, right? It is. Basic stuff can save lives!

And THAT'S how you hinder a haemorrhage!

COMMENTS: HEY TULIP, GREAT BLOG BUT YOU GOTTA STOP PUTTING PEOPLE'S NAMES IN THESE THINGS! ALSO, IT WASN'T JUST YOU.

ADMIN: HEY, YOU'RE RIGHT, SO SORRY, DIDN'T MEAN 2B A CREDIT GRABBER. DUDES, FORGOT TO SAY THAT MY

FRIENDS, JAY AND ZAC, HELPED TOO!

COMMENTS: SERIOUSLY, TULIP. YOU'RE HOPELESS.

COMMENTS 2: STOP TROLLING HER, NOOB. BTW JUST SENT YOU A VIDEO OF SOMEONE CALLED JAY FALLING INTO A PILE OF POO! LOL.

COMMENTS: ALI? YOU'RE HOPELESS, TOO.

TWINTERMISSION!
PLUMBERS AND ELECTRICIANS
AKA VASCULAR SURGEONS AND NEUROSURGEONS
AND WHY SURGEONS AREN'T CALLED DOCTOR!

So, Mum's a neurosurgeon, which means she's the sort of surgeon who deals with the neurology in your biology.

That means NERVES. They're the info cables of the body, there's no internal WiFi, it all goes down the hard wiring. And the wiring mostly starts in your brain, and spine, and then spreads out.

Mum fixes things that might stop the nerves working, like a big lump growing in your brain that's squashing them. She'll scrape it out, and check that everything's working while she's doing it. Quite often, people are awake during brain surgery, so they can tell you they're OK, and they're not suddenly hearing music because you nicked the auditory centre, or can't say the names for things, because you damaged that naming bit at the front.

Mum's friend, Miss Glory, is a vascular surgeon, a sort of body plumber. If the pipes carrying the blood around the body need fixing, or re-directing, she'll do that. Sometimes they can fix an artery by borrowing another bit of tubing, like a vein. There's no need to keep people awake during vascular surgery, they might get a bit freaked out by the blood!

And did you know, surgeons aren't called doctors! Miss Glory was Dr Glory when she finished med school, but now she's a consultant, which means top of the tree, like the headteacher at school, she's back to being a miss. That's because surgeons in the UK in the olden days didn't have to be doctors, but were tradesmen, like barbers or butchers, who learned by watching their boss at work. It's a bit confusing, as it means the med student watching the surgery has the same title as the top surgeon doing the slicing and dicing.

But not all doctors are medical doctors anyway, as if you have a PhD, or a doctorate in anything at all, like poetry or physics, you can call yourself a doctor. So it's worth asking what kind of doctor someone is, before asking them to look at your warts.

TWINTERMISSION!
BACTERIA HYSTERIA
OR THE PSEUDOMONAS EXPERIMENT

Bacteria are everywhere! Seriously. They're on your skin (Staph Aureus) and in your tum (E Coli), and that's OK, if that's where they're meant to be! The trouble is when a bacteria that's sitting happily on your foot gets into your bloodstream because you've got a nasty wound, and then it gets pretty mean, multiplies by doubling, and needs SERIOUS antibiotics to get rid of it.

The same goes with E Coli, which is quite chillaxed in your tum, but if it goes somewhere it's not meant to be, like the nicely sterile tube that you pee from, you can get a very icky infection.

THE EXPERIMENT

If you want to SEE bacteria in action, it's pretty easy. We do it all the time.

STEP 1: Just forget to do the washing up.

STEP 2: Then forget to do it again.

STEP 3: And then again.

Repeat Steps 1-3. And eventually there'll

be a green icky scum on the water. That's Pseudomonas! Big, beautiful, icky-sicky-scummy bacteria!

So when you haven't done the washing up, just tell your grown-up that you're doing science. Unless your grown-up is our mum, as she's already worked this one out. 🤢 🤮

COMMENTS: DUDES, WE SHOWED THIS TO MUM, AND SHE'S WORRIED ABOUT YOU, AND WANTS TO COME AROUND AND CLEAN YOUR KITCHEN. LIKE NOW. SHE SAYS SHE WON'T BE ABLE TO SLEEP.

ADMIN: AWW, YOUR MUM'S THE BEST! BUT DON'T WORRY. OUR MUM'S BANNED US FROM PSEUDOMONAS EXPERIMENTS FOR A WHILE. WE'RE GROWING MOULD ON BREAD, INSTEAD. THAT'S HOW YOU GET PENICILLIN.

Blood doctors are called haematologists. And there are basically three types of blood cells to know about.

● **RED BLOOD CELLS**—these look like red sweets with a squished-in centre, like little bowls. They're about forty per cent of your blood, and the most important thing they do is carry oxygen (the stuff you breathe in) around your body and unload the carbon dioxide (the stuff you breathe out) in your lungs.

● **WHITE BLOOD CELLS**—there are a few kinds of these, and they make up about one per cent of your blood. They race around and kill bacteria and viruses in the body.

●° **PLATELETS**—these are actually bits of bone marrow cells, but they get activated when the blood needs to clot. What's clotting? Think of Witch eating a bowl of cream that's spoonable, not pourable. That's clotted cream, basically cream that isn't liquid any more, but solid. So clotting means the blood stops being a liquid, and becomes a sticky solid mess, like if your knee is bleeding. Platelets stop the bleeding and let a scab form.

COMMENTS: BLOOD, BLOOD, BLOOD.

ADMIN: ALI, I KNOW THAT'S YOU.

COMMENTS: U CAN'T HEAR ME, COZ I'M WHISPERING IT . . . BLOOD, BLOOD, BLOOD.

ADMIN: SAY SORRY OR I'M SO GONNA BLOCK YOU.

COMMENTS: THAT'S SO MEAN! BTW, U KNOW WHAT RHYMES WITH HAEMATOLOGY?

ADMIN: APOLOGY?

COMMENTS: HAHAHA, YOU APOLOGIZED TO ME! AND I ACCEPT! NO BACKSIES.

Don't want to get all preachy and uncool here, but smoking straight up sucks.

It makes you sick. It costs you money and it makes you smell bad.

There is literally NO REASON to smoke, unless you like being sick, smelling bad, and having less money for cake.

It can KILL you too, most people with lung cancer get it from smoking. And if you smoke in the same house as your family, you can make THEM sick too.

So what do you do if someone you care about is blowing smoke? Help them to stop. Nicotine in cigarettes is seriously addictive, like eating sugar but worse, and it's really hard to give up, but the good news is that nicotine isn't that bad in itself, it's the little death sticks that are bad, so just try nicotine replacement gum or patches.

And once it's out of your system, don't go back.

So just remember, Smoking isn't smart! So

don't be the uncool dude who starts!

COMMENTS: AWESOME!

ADMIN: AW, ZAC, YOU'RE READING THE BLOG. THANK YOU! 😃

COMMENTS: HEY, WHAT DID THE BIG CHIMNEY SAY TO THE LITTLE CHIMNEY?

ADMIN: DUNNO

COMMENTS: YOU'RE 2 YOUNG 2 SMOKE. 😄 👏

ADMIN: 😶

COMMENTS: YEAH, I'LL BE GOING NOW.

TWINTERMISSION:
MINI GUIDE TO THE BITS OF YOUR BRAIN
OR WHAT HAPPENS WHEN YOU GET A
WHACK TO YOUR HEAD!

Here's a pic of your brain! This is where the magic happens! This is the stuff that makes you, you!

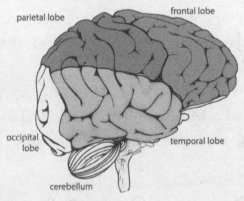

parietal lobe

frontal lobe

occipital lobe

temporal lobe

cerebellum

So the frontal lobes, the bits at the front, that's where you make decisions and if you get bashed there, you can completely change your personality. There was a guy who was quite sensible, but then he had a spike through his head in a work accident that took out a chunk of the frontal lobe, and he became really rude, behaved really badly and lived dangerously. All the brainy-bits that helped him make good decisions were gone.

The parietal lobes are about sorting out the information from your senses, taste and smell and touch, and science stuff like maths.

And the temporal lobes, the bits on the side, that's where memories are made, near your ears so they help you work out sound, like understanding language and listening to music.

And the occipital lobe, right at the back, helps you work out what you see. You can have working eyes, but still be 'brain-blind' if this bit isn't working.

That's why when we thought Sprotland could've had a bump on the head to change his personality, we knew it had to be a bump on the FRONT!

COMMENTS: HEY TULIP, SO COULD A BUMP ON THE FRONT OF THE HEAD TURN SOMEONE INTO A NICER PERSON? ASKING FOR A FRIEND.

ADMIN: UM, I GUESS.

COMMENTS 2: JAY, THAT YOU? 😳 WHICH FRIEND YOU TALKING ABOUT, NOOB?

COMMENTS: NO ONE, ALI. NO ONE AT ALL.

Thank you for visiting
the Mini-Medix Blog.
Come again!
#MiniMedix

A DOUBLE
DETECTIVES
MEDICAL MYSTERY

THE CURE FOR A CRIME

ROOPA FAROOKI

PATIENT: MUM (TRAINEE NEUROSURGEON,
NORMAL MUM-SKILLS GENERALLY GOOD.)

SYMPTOMS: WEIRDLY SLEEPY, CAN'T REMEMBER
ANYTHING, JUST NOT RIGHT.

DIAGNOSIS: SOMETHING DIABOLICAL.

Twins Ali and Tulip are worried
about their mum.
Ever since her new boyfriend moved in
it's like she's a different person.
Like she's been turned into a zombie robot.

And now Mum's sinister sleepy-sickness is
spreading . . . into school.
A strange infection . . . or criminal intention?
The double detectives are on the case!
Can Ali and Tulip solve this mystery before
it's too late . . . ?

ACKNOWLEDGEMENTS:

I was editing this book during the Covid-19 pandemic, working into the night as an NHS frontline doctor, looking after patients in A&E and the ward. Like many of my colleagues, I contracted Covid-19 while caring for those with the virus. I didn't need to go into hospital for specialist treatment, I survived, but many were not so lucky.

So this is for my heroic NHS colleagues and frontline key-workers, who prove that real heroes don't wear capes, they are the ones who care, showing compassion and kindness in their daily work.

The contribution of BAME medics and staff to the NHS has never been more obvious, and I'm so happy to have written a series with BAME medics featured proudly on the covers. Thank you to the incredible team at Oxford University Press for making this happen.

And with love to my four children, Alia, Zarena, Zaki and Jaan, who lit up these medical mysteries, with their curiosity, mischief, laughter and bickering. You inspire me every day.

ABOUT THE AUTHOR

Roopa Farooki is a junior doctor working for the NHS in London and Kent. She has four children (twin girls and two boys).

Roopa is also the award-winning author of six literary novels for adults, that have been published in over twenty countries, and has been listed for the Women's Prize for Fiction three times. She received an Arts Council Award and Author's Foundation Prize for work that increases understanding between cultures. She lectures in creative writing at the University of Oxford, is a Royal Literary Fund Fellow and is the Ambassador for Family for the relationship charity, Relate.

She says that doctors, detectives and writers have something in common, they all like to solve mysteries, and work out what makes people tick.

@RoopaFarooki

Here are some other stories we think you'll love...